NEPHILIM

JOHN BARROWMAN is an entertainer with a career that includes theatre, television, music and film. He is currently Malcolm Merlyn in *Arrow*, *Legends of Tomorrow* and *The Flash*. He is acclaimed for his portrayal of Captain Jack in *Torchwood* and *Doctor Who*.

CAROLE E. BARROWMAN, is an English professor and Director of Creative Studies in Writing at Alverno College in Milwaukee, Wisconsin, where she also writes a column on crime fiction for the *Milwaukee Journal Sentinel*, and reviews for the *Minneapolis Star Tribune*.

The siblings have collaborated on seven books and a number of comics.

For more on their work go to www.barrowmanbooks.com

JOHN & CAROLE BARROWMAN

NEPHILIM

HEAD
of ZEUS

9 7 5 3 1 2 4 6 8

A catalogue record for this book is available from the British Library.

ISBN (HB): 9781781856413
ISBN (E): 9781781856406

Typeset by Adrian McLaughlin

Printed and bound in Great Britain by CPI Group (UK) Ltd, Croydon CR0 4YY

Head of Zeus Ltd
First Floor East
5–8 Hardwick Street
London EC1R 4RG
WWW.HEADOFZEUS.COM

NEPHILIM

*To our mum and dad, Marion and John,
and to bags, shoes, fine wine and
the pool at Palm Springs*

'A true compendium of conjurations, invocations, curses and the mystical instruments that...

...Behold the Watchers, God's angels who fell from chaos. One day their kingdom will rule the earth... only a Conjuror shall cull them...

And Behold the Conjuror shall be exalted
For he shall play the sacred chord...
and with the divine instrument of the Lord
the dead will...'

Book of Songs

'Awake, arise or be for ever fall'n.'

—JOHN MILTON, *Paradise Lost*

FIRST MOVEMENT

'[The Watchers] ... rejected the Lord of light,
and after them are those who are held in
great darkness on the second heaven...'

The Book of Enoch

1.

FORBIDDEN
FRUIT

ITALY, 1610

Michelangelo Merisi de Caravaggio knew he was dying. The stab wound had seen to that. But, in the height of his fever, all he could think about was peaches.

'Never eaten a peach,' he gasped as the carriage bumped and swayed along the rutted track. 'A dying shame. A peach like a fine arse that I could sink my teeth into. Never … never tasted a peach…'

'And I've never tasted the Queen of France,' snorted a fellow traveller, a sour cobbler from Florence reeking of tannin and shit, who sucked in his pockmarked cheeks and let the air whistle out through missing teeth. 'Don't see that happening any time soon either.' He laughed, the cackle dislodging something rotten, which he hocked out through the open window.

A handsome young Highlander with striking blue eyes and skin as pale as a maiden's veil leaned forward in his seat. 'Sir,' he said in sketchy Italian. 'Have some respect for Queen Catherine.'

'Listen, *scutese*,' sneered the cobbler, spitting into his hand and wiping the phlegm on the Highlander's muscular kilted thigh. 'I've respect for two things in this world: Florentine leather, and death. And since one's having its way with your friend, you'd best get out of my business and look to his.'

The Highlander rested his hand casually on the cobbler's knee. The cobbler slumped over on the straw-stuffed seat, farted and began snoring noisily.

'Save your magic, *scutese*,' said Caravaggio, smiling through his pain.

'Ach, I've enough for us both.' The Highlander regarded Caravaggio soberly, peeling an orange from his bag. 'Michele, you should have relayed your message to us sooner, and come to Era Mina and safety. Before the Camarilla discovered you.'

'*Mio amico*,' Caravaggio gasped. 'Had I known such a place existed, I would have been there years ago, bedding your wife.'

'And if I had a wife, you'd be in my stockades by now. But at least you'd be safe.'

A coughing fit wrenched at Caravaggio's fever-wracked body, and he spat blood on to the layer of straw on the carriage's plank floor, the stony ground visible through the gashes in the rotting wood. Lifting a pouch from beneath his wide tartan sash, the Highlander passed his wine across. The artist had no energy to reach for it. He was barely able to sit upright. Quickly, the Highlander kneeled in front of him, holding the pouch to his lips.

'Drink, man,' he instructed. 'We've a long journey ahead.'

Caravaggio gulped the wine, dribbling most of it down his chin as the Highlander gently dabbed his lips with the sleeve of his tunic. 'Are they close behind us, do you think?' he croaked.

'The smoke we saw as we left the tavern was theirs. But if we're lucky, we'll make it to Manciano before they catch us.'

'And what … what if I'm wrong?' Caravaggio fretfully moved the leather folios packed with his canvases into a more secure position beneath his feet. 'What if I am mad?'

In the fading darkness of his mind, he heard again the murmurings from his models in Naples. How no one wanted to stay in the Cardinal's palace after dark. How no one wanted to walk through the galleries alone. And then those hellish abominations struggling out from a vast canvas while the Cardinal and his household rocked on their knees in prayer before them.

The Highlander snorted. 'Don't be daft, man. You're not mad, you're an Animare.'

Caravaggio closed his eyes. 'Animare,' he whispered to himself, as spasms of pain ripped him from side to side. 'Yes. My brush can truly bring things to life... Peaches...'

'What you witnessed proves what the Council of Guardians have long suspected,' said the Highlander. 'That the Camarilla have reached the highest levels of the state and the church. If we are to stop them, we must risk exposing ourselves to achieve it.' The cobbler's head flopped on to the Highlander's shoulder. He flicked him away. 'And if we are to gather our forces to fight against their rise, we must get you and the canvas to safety first.'

Caravaggio nodded through a haze of pain. His fingers started sketching, almost of their own accord, steadying the piece of charcoal in his fingers against his raised knee and the rocking of the carriage, his hands shaking from even such modest exertion.

'Save your strength, man.' The Highlander stretched his long legs across the space between them, folding the heavy pleats of his great kilt between his knees. 'My magic can only take us so far. Ah'm going tae need your help to get us to the north.'

In a starry burst of light, a peach fell out of the air. Caravaggio caught it in his trembling hands and bit down. He gagged when a writhing mass of maggots gushed from the ripe fruit.

2.

FIRE AND
BRIMSTONE

The freshly painted pink village sat on the lip of a Tuscan hillside. Every cottage, outhouse and barn had been washed in pink to celebrate the coming midsummer solstice. The landscape resembled a fairy-tale wedding cake baked into the clay.

Blue flames licked the walls of the tavern in the heart of the village, lapped across the thatched roof and snaked inside. Men shouted, women screamed and children wailed. In seconds, the air was choked with the stench of sulphur and seared flesh. It smelled like evil.

Luca Ferrante, the Imperial Commander of the Camarilla, tugged on the reins of his terrified horse until its mouth bled, observing the chaos from afar. Even from this distance, the stench was overpowering. He licked his full, rose-red lips and played with the curls falling loosely over his shoulders, listening to the faint trill of flute music die out until only the cry of a hawk and the bark of a wild dog rose above the hissing and spitting of the smouldering ruins. The rising sun slowly bathed the Tuscan hillside in swathes of burned orange and cherry red. Luca cupped his eyes with his black-gloved hand, enjoying the irony that in its darkest moment, the village was bathed in light.

The enjoyment was short-lived. For all the glory of destruction, he still did not have what he wanted. He had been riding for two days, only stopping once to feed and water his horse, in the firm belief that he would catch this prey during the first daylight of the hunt. Instead his stomach growled, his head ached, his buttocks were bruised, and his temper was simmering. All his sacrifices were beginning to feel like empty gestures. The painting of the Cardinal was safe en route to the New World, but now the artist had escaped with the sacred chord. Without that, the rise of the Watchers would be forever impossible.

Would he ever see his glory attained?

Luca had already experienced chaos, rebellion, anarchy and betrayal in his long existence. But the Second Kingdom would remain a prophecy if he did not retrieve what the artist had stolen. Luca was a soldier. He must not fail. He stifled his doubts and swallowed his anger. Both were emotions too human to let surface.

A movement caught his eye at the convent of the Hermits of St Augustine on the peak above the village. A young nun, barefoot, pressing the hem of her black shift to her face, was sprinting across the convent's cobbled courtyard as the stench and the smoke wound greasily over the convent walls. The courtyard was cracked and jagged, and if Luca held his head at a slight angle, he could catch the smell of blood from the pads of her feet.

At the heavy oak door set into the high convent wall, the young nun urged the last cluster of straggling villagers inside, then leaned against the door until it closed with a thunderclap that echoed down the valley.

Luca smiled sourly at the girl's spirit as he rode down the hill and into the village. Such a shame it wouldn't last. Her world would crumble soon.

3.

A TASTE OF EVIL

The fire had not spread beyond the tavern. The other dwellings in the village were shuttered and silent. A tribe of goats grazed on the sparse scrub, oblivious to the smoke teasing its way towards them, but the fire remained contained. Luca made sure of that. He loved the Tuscan countryside too much to lay it to waste.

A wild dog snarled from the cover of a vegetable cart as Luca's horse trotted along the dusty road, adding to the cacophony of screams and howls from the tavern. Luca caught the dog's eye and growled softly. The dog yelped and shot away. Luca tugged at his agitated stallion's reins as steam snorted from its flared nostrils. It, too, tasted the evil.

Soon the ticking of flames and the snapping of wood from the intense heat were the only sounds remaining. Ash was falling from the summer sky in big grey flakes. Luca took off his glove and held out his hand, letting the dust fill his palm. He rubbed it between his fingers and inhaled its scent like an exotic spice.

'Where are you, my rakish Animare?' he murmured. 'My handsome thief?'

He slipped his glove back on, his anger rising again. He looked back at the scrub and the goats. A rider dressed in silver chainmail similar to Luca's own galloped across the field and leaped over the startled goats, kicking up sod as his horse took the hedges in one athletic leap. Corso Donati pulled up next to Luca, the golden lyre of the Camarilla billowing on his purple cloak in the smoky air.

'I freed the village horses, sir,' Corso informed his master, stroking his horse's neck and soothing its nerves as it paced a safe distance from the Imperial Commander.

Luca nodded. It would be a shame to see such noble beasts suffer more than necessary. He turned his attention back to the tavern at the end of the road. 'And the artist? Tell me, Corso, that you have the artist.'

Corso's hand trembled on his restive horse's mane. 'It appears he has escaped. Again.'

'His wounds were fatal,' said Luca. 'How has he survived this far? His injuries alone should have killed him, never mind the ride from Rome.'

'He must be a more powerful Animare than we believed. Or he has help.'

Luca's cold blue eyes were slits. He nursed the vision of Michelangelo Merisi de Caravaggio crying out in passion under his hand. He should have known that the artist's flesh was weak and his motives not to be trusted. 'Corpse or not, he'll be mine soon enough.'

They trotted closer to the tavern's smoke-filled yard and smouldering hitching posts. Most of the four walls remained standing, but the second floor and its bunks of straw had collapsed into the interior of the structure. The smell of burned flesh tickled Luca's nostrils.

'The innkeeper told me the artist fled before sunrise,' Corso informed his master.

'Has he told you anything more?'

'No. He is … uncooperative.'

Luca tightened his grip on his horse's reins. 'The chord?'

'Still in the artist's possession.'

'The Animare must not get away,' hissed Luca. 'We must find him. I tire of this filthy world. I am weary of its undisciplined magic. I need rest.'

Animare were a necessary evil. They allowed the Camarilla to build wealth beyond what any man, monarch, nation, state or pope would ever realize. Luca understood that better than anyone. But although Animare and their talents afforded him a way to move in and out of the world, he distrusted their motives. Even those who were loyal raised his ire. Too many of them worshipped their art above all else. And they placed far too much faith in humanity. That would, in the end, prove to be their downfall. Of that he had no doubt.

'You're sure of the route the artist has taken?' he asked, climbing from his horse and handing the reins to his squire.

'The carriage is travelling to Manciano, sir. The duke promised the artist sanctuary with an order of Jesuit brothers less than a day's ride from here. We'll have him and the chord before sundown.' Corso turned his horse and trotted towards the outskirts of the village.

Luca strode closer to the dying flames, shielding his face from the heat. He quietened his thoughts. Let his focus return.

He cast the net with his mind.

Where are you?

A whisper returned on the breeze.

I am here.

A spectacular flash of blue and yellow flames forked across the tavern like sheet lightning. For a second Luca saw his true self in the flames: a beautiful beast with full black wings stippled with silver, rippling with energy and power.

A woman in a scarlet gown cinched at the waist glided out of the charred carcass of the building. Her bronze skin shone. Ash streaked her jet-black hair. She held a sword in her right hand, and in her left the dripping, severed head of the innkeeper. Luca's heart filled with love: the kind about which humans write poetry, the kind that scorches a soul. The kind he had hungered for his whole life.

The woman raised the innkeeper's head and opened her mouth to drink his fire-warm blood. Flames shot up her back, snapping at her hair. Stirred from his lustful thoughts, Luca threw himself on her, knocking her to the ground. They rolled across the yard in a frenzied embrace until the flames sputtered out.

'You are a dangerous one, Sebina,' said Luca, before kissing her hard on the lips.

Sebina lifted herself off Luca's chest, brushed his hair from his face. 'Luca, my angel,' she purred. 'I had everything under control.'

4.

FATES BE DAMNED

'You should take your leave, *scutese*. My fate is sealed, but you do not need to be locked in it with me.'

The stab wound in Caravaggio's side wept, blood staining his tattered tunic. The skin under his eyes looked like pellets of dough and the slash wound across his face had opened. It, too, was weeping.

'Fates be damned,' said the Highlander.

The carriage was hurtling north as fast as its horses could manage. Each time a wheel caught the edge of a rut, pain exploded through every bone in Caravaggio's body. He didn't have much time left.

'If I had been thinking rationally,' he gasped, 'I would have done things differently.'

'Regrets are like scorned lovers,' said the Highlander. 'To revisit them is dangerous.'

The cobbler let out a loud belch, scratched his balls and rolled on to his side. He would have tumbled out of the carriage if the Highlander hadn't gripped him by his collar and hauled him back inside.

'You're lucky the Moor was in Calais when he contacted us,' said the Highlander, settling the cobbler more securely. 'Otherwise, it would have been impossible for me to reach Rome in time.'

Caravaggio picked up the folio containing his rolled canvases, wrapping his arms around them. They did nothing to staunch the bleeding. His spirit was weakening, resistance seeping out through his pores. Sweat dripped down his back, yet he was shivering. The Highlander reached over and took his hand.

'Your skin is cold,' he said gently. 'And your pulse faint. You must rest, my friend. You must sleep.'

At the Highlander's touch, the artist's pulse steadied and his eyelids fluttered. The Highlander caressed the artist's bruised knuckles in rhythm to the smack of the carriage's wheels on the steep mountain pass. Caravaggio lifted his battered head in a last bid for consciousness, bits of peach flesh still caught between his teeth.

'*Scutese*, my friend, my saviour,' he whispered. 'I never asked your name.'

The Highlander smiled. 'Mason Renard Calder, the fourth Duke of Albion and Knight of the Order of Era Mina, at your service.'

5.

FALSE CRUSADERS

The Duke of Albion closed Caravaggio's sketchbook and slipped it into his sporran. Then he laid the artist on his back on the lumpy straw and attempted to loosen his grip on the canvases. The artist groaned, embracing the folio like a long-lost lover.

The carriage began to slow, the climb stretching the limits of the horses. A flash of light cut into the duke's mind. He parted the carriage curtain just enough to see three riders approaching on two horses, cresting the hill behind them. All of them wore the military dress of the Camarilla, its golden herald emblazoned on their cloaks.

They had caught up faster than the duke had hoped. These false crusaders would drag the artist back to Rome, where his fate would be sealed with the stroke of an axe or flames at the stake. Either way, death would greet him in the morning.

Unless.

'Up, my friend,' said the duke, shaking the artist as hard as he dared.

Caravaggio's head lolled back on his chest. The wagon lurched. The riders bounded closer. The duke cursed the strength of his own magic. His inspiriting had put the artist in too deep a sleep, and neither he nor the cobbler would rouse.

The duke finally pried the canvases from Caravaggio's arms and slipped the folio strap over his head. He lifted the artist to his knees and propped him against the door. Frantically, he flipped through the canvases until he found the one he had been sent to seize and protect. He gazed at the painting for a moment, marvelling at the artist's skill. Tucking it safely away inside his shirt, he poured his remaining ale over the rest, heartsick as the rush of liquid ruined the glory of these final works.

The carriage struggled on up the rocky pass.

'Halt! In the name of the Holy Father!'

'Do not heed them,' yelled the duke to the driver. 'I'll triple the fee we promised.'

The driver struck his horses and the carriage speeded up, but the duke knew it would not be enough. He looked out of the carriage window again.

The lead rider was clearly a squire, his sword raised as he charged ahead of his master. But it was the two riders sharing the black stallion behind that drew the duke's interest most. The sun glinted off the knight's blond hair and his cloak flared out behind him, almost engulfing one of the most beautiful women the Highlander had ever seen. A hand gripped his heart and a knot twisted in his gut.

Sebina.

He recognized her from sketches locked in the vault at the Abbey in Scotland. If Sebina was in the world, then the knight with her had to be the Imperial Commander of the Camarilla, Sebina's lover, much more and much worse. The duke cursed. Of course the Camarilla would call forth the best. Whatever Caravaggio had hidden in the canvas now nestling against his heart was worth releasing Lucius Ferrante into this world. The duke could not let the painting get into their hands.

Not ever.

6.

APOLOGIES,
MY FRIEND

The duke kicked open the carriage door. He waited until it thundered through some trees and alongside a steep ravine, below which lay a thin line of blue. 'Forgive me, friend,' he whispered.

He hefted the artist out of the carriage and watched as the limp body crashed through the brush and disappeared down the ravine. The duke hurled the sodden leather folio after him, and heard it splash.

The carriage raced on. The duke sliced the sleeping cobbler's throat with a grimace. It was unfortunate, but the Camarilla would do worse to the man if they thought he was a witness.

The riders were on the carriage's tail now.

'Halt!'

The duke pulled straw from the seat and spread it across the other bench. Then he climbed into the resulting nest and, with all his upper-body strength, pulled the dead cobbler on top of him. The man's blood and stink seeped into the straw. The duke burrowed deeper, adjusting his position to let the blood fill the spaces. Finally, he tore a piece of cloth from the back of the cobbler's jacket and covered his face with it. It reeked of sweat and iron.

The carriage hit a rock and almost flipped before skidding to a halt, the horses bucking.

'Step down, curse you!'

From his coffin in the straw, the duke heard the telltale swoosh of a sword sliding from its scabbard. He noted the snap of fallen branches as someone walked towards the carriage. He cringed as a blade sliced through the driver's neck and a body thudded to the ground outside the door.

He held his breath.

He silenced his thoughts.

He believed in magic, not miracles, but he found himself praying for the prophecy. Now would be an excellent time for the promised Conjuror to make himself known.

7.

A LINGERING SEDUCTION

As casually as tearing a page from a manuscript, Luca ripped the carriage door from its hinges and leaned into the stench of blood and shit. He ducked his head and climbed inside, stabbed his sword into the seat where Caravaggio had been and sat down. He poked the dead man's belly with the silver tip of his snakeskin boot. The body belched.

He faced the stinking corpse with a sense of disquiet. There was something strange and slightly seductive lingering in the carriage, like a hint of perfume on a lover's pillow or the scent of terror in the air before a battle. Luca inhaled desperation and disgust, fear and dread.

Sebina floated into view at the broken carriage door, a sodden leather folio in her hands.

'It seems that he jumped from the carriage and drowned. There's a visible trail through the brush, ending at the shore, but the undertow is strong and the tide has dispatched any real evidence.' She stepped delicately inside the carriage. 'Corso has ridden on to the Jesuit church, in the event that he did escape.'

'He had help,' said Luca. His blue eyes narrowed. 'Someone else was attending to him in this carriage. I can feel the presence of a Guardian. A powerful one.'

'Him?' asked Sebina in amusement, prodding at the body.

'Not this fool.'

'The Moor, then?'

'My spies tell me the Moor has found sanctuary in the north. We will deal with him ... eventually.'

Sebina sat, stretching her legs out to rest on Luca's lap. He caressed her bare feet. She moaned and leaned back against the torn upholstery. Loosening a bloody stalk from the straw beneath her, she held it against her throat and traced a line down her breastbone. The moment the blood touched her skin, her neck became translucent, absorbing the whisper of life like a drop of water on fine silk.

'How long must we hunt the Animare?' she asked. 'This place, this time, bores me.'

Luca watched the throbbing pulse at the curve of Sebina's long neck as her skin darkened again to its natural bronze. 'As long as it takes. Time, after all, is a mere mortal construct.'

He slipped his sword into its sheath at his side and stepped down from the carriage, holding his hand out to

Sebina. As she reached to take it, she paused and looked at the saturated bench of hay beneath the corpse.

'What is it?' asked Luca.

Sebina uncovered a brooch caught in the straw. She held it up to the light streaming in through the rear of the carriage.

'Beautiful,' she said, dropping it into Luca's cupped hand, before stepping into the midday sun.

The brooch was shaped like a flying stag, the detail so delicate it made the feathering of its wings look real. It had been carved from a piece of polished green stone flecked with drops of red. Bloodstone. Luca's own bloodlust rose.

'Bloodstone,' he said. 'One of the most powerful elements in an alchemist's inventory.' He leaped back into the carriage, his sword pointing at the cobbler. The corpse stiffened at his touch. Luca sniffed the air once more, quashed the fear suddenly rising in his breast. 'And this beast is the symbol of the Knights of Era Mina,' he said, forcing out the words. 'I must report to Rome immediately. They will not be pleased that Era Mina is involved.'

Sebina pouted. 'What about Corso?'

'He will follow.'

'And me?'

Luca jumped lightly out of the carriage again. 'My love, you will remain at my side.'

The ground beneath their feet cracked and shuddered

as Sebina put her lips on his and kissed him deeply. Luca's body rose off the ground, his flesh melting, becoming thicker, darker, scalier. Double black wings infused with silver light unfolded around Sebina as Luca tipped back his head, his thick curls flaming out behind him. Sebina melted against his muscular, bestial form.

We will endure.

8.

A CELESTIAL SINGULARITY

PRESENT DAY

Before dawn on the summer solstice, an alarming apparition appeared above a tiny, medieval church deep in the Scottish highlands. The flickering phantasm curled and coiled and curved around the church's ancient spire like a silent banshee.

Minutes later, the neon-green spectre was stretching across the fields towards the nearest hamlet, Kentigern, on the edge of the Cairngorm National Park and tucked beneath the ruins of St Mungo's Castle.

Standing at her kitchen window, Collyn Lambert was pouring milk on her four-year-old daughter's cereal when she noticed the ghostly stream coming from the church on the hillside and looping over her neighbours' roofs. She put the bowl and a slice of jammy toast in front of Mabel, went out to the cottage's narrow hall, and yelled upstairs to her husband.

'Do you see that weird light outside, Alex?'

'Ah'm changing Ben in the bathroom!' her husband called back. 'All ah can see is shite. This wee man can fill a diaper.'

'It looks like a UFO!'

'Mummy,' piped up Mabel. 'I want to see.'

It was not yet six o'clock, but the sky was ablaze with light. Collyn could hear the wind brushing the trees, and in the distance one or two cars heading out to the main road. Just like every morning since they'd moved here from Fife. Except for that peculiar light.

She carried Mabel to the middle of the lawn and watched in awe as the ribbons of light rippled over the roofs towards the castle, where they were gathering in a halo around the ruins.

'Why would aliens want to land up here?' asked Alex from the doorstep, Ben nestled on his hip.

'For our whisky?' Collyn carried Mabel back inside, pinching her husband's bottom as she passed him. 'For our men?'

'Ha,' said Alex, closing the back door and setting Ben on the floor next to a line of toy police cars and fire engines. 'If they take our whisky, then they might as well take me too, right, Ben?'

'Nee naw, nee naw,' replied Ben, whizzing a police car between the legs of the kitchen table and crashing it into the dishwasher on the other side.

'What do you think the light really is?' Collyn said,

an anxious flutter in her words, a knot tightening in her stomach. 'It's beginnin' tae creep me out.'

Mabel said something, but neither of her parents heard her. Because all at once the landline rang, both their mobiles vibrated angrily on the butcher's-block table, someone thumped menacingly on their front door, and Ben began to cry.

'Too loud!' he sobbed, holding his hands to his ears. 'Too loud!'

Collyn silenced the shrill on the landline and reached for her mobile, noticing a long thread of texts from her neighbours. The mobile pulsed in her clammy hand.

'Don't answer the door,' she said, looking up. 'Something bad's happening.'

'Ach, rubbish,' replied Alex as he went to open it.

Ben stopped screaming abruptly.

'Sweetie,' said Collyn, tugging at the Cheerios caught in the tugs of Mabel's reddish-blond hair, 'what did you just say to Mummy a wee minute ago?'

Mabel pointed at the glow outside the window. 'I think the light sounds really nice.'

'Me too,' said Ben, driving a fire truck into his mum's hip.

9.

HOOLIGANS AND HIPPIES

'I think those bloody hippies up in the auld kirk are up tae somethin',' said Gordon Cross, marching into the kitchen. 'I've always said a cult bought the church and a' that land.' He mussed Mabel's hair as he headed to the window. 'Or maybe it's a sex-trafficking ring?'

Alex rolled his eyes and grabbed his overcoat from the hook in the mudroom.

'Gordon,' said Collyn. 'The kids...'

'You've seen how young those new recruits are,' continued Gordon, tapping his fingers aggressively on the sink as he watched the light dance across the trees outside. 'Not much older than my Morag.'

'Your Morag's eighteen, she's an adult, and so are those kids up there,' said Alex, kissing the top of Mabel's head and Ben's sticky cheek. 'It's not a cult.'

'Aye, well, yer being too trusting. In my day we would've marched right up there...'

'Torches in hand...' added Alex.

Gordon snorted. 'That's no' natural, that light. If you ask me, it's witchcraft. Dark magic.'

Collyn pulled out a chair at the table, brushing crumbs from it. 'Gordon, sit,' she instructed. 'You'll work yourself up to a stroke if you don't calm down. You know right well it's not a cult. They train art restorers for museums, and they've been good to the village. If it weren't for them, we wouldn't have the swing park or the football fields.'

'They're pagans,' grumbled Gordon. 'Or hippies.' He leaned over and zoomed the toy police car back under the table to Ben. 'And ma mind's no' that addled yet, is it, wee man?'

'Says you,' replied Alex, filling a flask with coffee.

'Wheesht the both of you.' Collyn absently registered the way Mabel's hand was cupped conspiratorially against Ben's ear, whispering to him. 'The auld kirk hasn't been a real church in centuries, and I'd rather have artists up there than drunk grammar-school students, that's for sure.'

'All ah'm saying is that someone should report it,' said Gordon.

'I'll do it on my way to work,' said Alex, lifting his briefcase from the bottom of the stairs beneath a pile of dirty laundry.

Collyn followed her husband to the door. 'If you call it in, love,' she said as Alex kissed her goodbye, 'make sure it's someone other than Constable Bill. Honestly, that man's a clown.'

It was still dark outside, and the glow from the eerie light was bathing everything in a kind of phosphorescent yellow. Collyn decided she'd call one of the scientists at the university herself once she got rid of Gordon and settled the kids in front of *Peppa Pig* for twenty minutes. There must be a scientific reason for the light. The *aurora borealis*, or something like that.

On her way back down the hall, she picked up two toys and random pieces of clothing from the floor. But when she stepped back into the kitchen, she dropped them all.

Gordon was lying on his back on the tiles, blood oozing from a bad cut on his forehead.

'The weans,' he whispered, pointing to the back gate. 'Sorry … I … I tried to stop them...'

Panic clutching at her chest, Collyn scanned the cluttered garden. 'Mabel? Ben?' she called. Above her head, the ribbons of light were dimming as the sun was rising over the distant Cairngorms. 'Where are you? WHERE ARE YOU?'

10.

DON'T BLAME ME

Inside the church tower, Em woke with a start and a horrible taste in her mouth. The air in her room crackled with a peculiar energy. She didn't need to look outside the arched window to know something weird was happening. She could feel the bizarre in her bones, taste the trouble on her tongue. Like sour milk and vinegar.

She rubbed at her hair until it stuck up in thick, pink-streaked tufts. She eyed herself in the mirror that hung on the plain white walls of her cell-like room.

'Hey there, trouble,' she murmured, scrunching her nose and her emerald-green eyes at her reflection. 'How's banishment looking today?'

In the darkest moments of her childhood, Em had thought the Council of Guardians were right to enforce the First Rule preventing Animare and Guardians from having kids. Particularly when her dad turned out to be such a monster. Now she was older, she knew the First

Rule was archaic and heartless and rooted in fear. If she hadn't broken Zach Butler's heart and torn a black hole in his soul, they might have had kids some day. Councils be damned.

Em liked to think of Orion as MI5 for the supernatural. The organization had kept her and her twin brother Matt busy watching out for their kind for a while now, and the work was rewarding. But still, banishment was banishment. Even if Orion preferred the word 'reassignment'.

Em peered out of the tiny tower window at the giant, freaky slime monster circling the sky above the Highlands. It was a hell of a way to start the day.

The tower shook violently, knocking her easel over. The half-finished portrait of Zach fell face down on her bed and the paint pots she'd left open spilled on to the rug. She scrambled off the narrow bunk, ignoring the spill and lunging for the portrait. The rug already looked like a Jackson Pollock reject.

The taste in her mouth was getting worse, like she'd been sick during the night. Em gulped from the tap at the tiny porcelain sink in the corner. It didn't help. Pulling a bulky Aran-knit cardigan over her green T-shirt and yoga pants, she rushed down the narrow spiral stairs two at a time, and crashed out into the chill.

Directly into Matt, who was already outside. Taller than his sister, Matt was in skinny jeans, a vintage red Sex Pistols T-shirt and his ever-present Ray-Bans. He grabbed Em's shoulders before she fell backwards.

'What did you just dream about?' he demanded.

'Me?' protested Em, glancing at the neon lights swirling around the church and its courtyard as if a million invisible hands were waving green sparklers in the air. 'Why must you always blame me for the crazy stuff? Just because you and Zach had to kill a sexy Viking once in the kitchen, you've never let me forget it.'

'What about the professor from Hogwarts who almost stabbed Zach? Or Storm who almost flooded the backyard?'

'OK,' admitted Em. 'Maybe two or three times in my childhood I lost control of my animations and dreams and brought something interesting to the table. But not this time. I swear this has nothing to do with me.'

The swirling green light dipped towards them, and without thinking Em thrust her hand into it. Almost at once she gasped and whipped her hand out.

'It feels like it's sobbing,' she said, the intense emotion still running through her.

'Smart,' Matt said sarcastically. 'That thing could have taken your hand off. Maybe we could draw a container and trap it?'

'Maybe you should do your crocodile eyelid thing.'

'I do not have crocodile eyes,' said Matt with dignity. 'I have historical visions.'

'Historical vision, croc vision, whatever,' said Em. 'Try rewinding.'

Matt took off his shades. His eyes were always

seductive and stunning, weirdly mesmerizing and darkly troubling all at once, a constantly shifting kaleidoscope of colours and light: the consequence of time-travel gone wrong when he was much younger.

'There's too much light. I can't,' he said, and dropped his shades back on to his nose. Crouching and using the charcoal crayon he always kept to hand, he started sketching a cage on the flagged stones under their feet. But before he could finish it, Em wiped it away with the toe of her boot and pointed out over the village tucked into the valley beneath them.

'It's reached all the way to the castle ruins,' she said. 'No way a cage is going to cover that distance.'

'What about washing it out of the sky?'

He started to draw a hose. Em scuffed the ground again.

'Now you're just being ridiculous,' she said.

Matt shrugged. 'Well, we'd better think of something before more than just a few folks in the village see it.'

11.

TAKE THAT, MOZART

Moments later, Rémy sprinted out of the tower, almost tripping over Matt.

'What the hell is that?' he panted, staring at the light stretching out over the countryside. 'Not something good, I'm guessing. Is it yours, Em?'

Em glared.

'It's usually Animare who cause this sort of stuff,' Rémy pointed out.

Em prodded him in the chest. 'Just because you've been dancing with us cheek to cheek for a while doesn't mean you understand everything about Animare.'

'Woah,' Rémy said. 'Only looking for an explanation.'

'I could say the same thing about your T-shirt. Did you get dressed in the dark?'

Rémy looked down at himself. His faded hometown Chicago Bulls T-shirt was on backwards.

'Take that, Mozart,' Matt said.

Rémy had always heard the world in riffs and melodies,

in chords and notes, and sometimes in screams and howls. But it wasn't until his mother's murder that he'd appreciated the full extent of his reality-altering abilities. His imagination came with a streaming soundtrack.

Things had got better since joining Orion, but the creatures who'd killed his mother were hunting him now. He still missed her, hearing her voice in his head like background music.

'We'd better find out fast what's causing this spectre before someone higher up our food chain decides it *is* my fault and comes looking for us,' said Em.

Rémy scanned their surroundings. The church was older than America itself, with its two wooden doors, its arched windows and heavy old blockwork. He studied the light spiralling up from the tower. Listened. And heard a piccolo playing a jaunty jig with a creepy, calming tone.

'This is going to sound crazy,' he said, rubbing his brown eyes, 'but I think the light is playing music. And it's giving me a headache.'

'I've heard crazier,' said Matt, his Ray-Bans reflecting the eerie green light.

Em darted towards the great double doors that led into the nave, parting a way through the ribbons of dipping, darting light. Rémy ran to cut her off, planting himself in front of the doors.

'I don't think we should go inside,' he said. The pain was making him squint, and he struggled to put the sensation into words. 'It sounds as if the church is breathing.'

'That can't be good,' said Matt, twisting his thick curly hair into a knot at his neck.

Em pulled her cardigan tighter. 'So what do you suggest we do? You know what this kind of light means.'

'What?' asked Rémy, shading his eyes from the swirling spectre.

'Something powerful has animated inside the church.'

Matt slid his shades up on to his head. His eyes were on fire, brighter than Rémy had seen before.

'A little warning, Matt,' he said with a wince. 'Your eyes are a marching band full-tilt in my head.'

'We're the only ones in the compound right now who can animate.' Em paused. 'We are, right?'

'As far as I know,' said Matt.

The phantasm pulsed brighter, taunting them, swooping over the church roof above them. Em reached for the bronze door handle on the double doors leading into the nave. The handle was shaped like a flying stag: a peryton.

'I'm going in,' she said.

Rémy put his hand on top of Em's. A shock of electricity coursed through him, and he pulled away.

'There's something going on here that we don't understand,' said Matt, noticing Rémy's reaction. 'I think we should draw something first. A weapon, maybe.'

'Like what?' said Em, rubbing her hand. 'We don't know what we're up against.'

Almost without realizing, Rémy pulled his harmonica

from his pocket, wiping it on his thigh. 'You might make things worse,' he said.

'Thanks for the pep talk,' said Matt. 'Wait here.'

He hitched up his jeans and clambered on to a window ledge above them, his fingers feeling for fissures in the ancient stone, his toes digging into two deep crevices.

'Matt.' Em hissed as her brother scrambled up and over the guttering, which creaked beneath his weight. 'Have you lost your mind? I could've animated a ladder.'

Ignoring his sister, Matt climbed up the roof towards a skylight and was quickly lost inside the swirling green apparition.

Rémy stood on tiptoes and cupped his hands against the light, pressing his face against the small leaded-glass windowpane.

'Anything?' Em asked.

Rémy shook his head. Then without warning he collapsed to his knees, covering his ears with his hands. 'Aaargh!' he gasped. 'Can you hear that? Man, that hurts.'

'I don't hear anything,' said Em, kneeling next to him, 'but I can taste liquorice. Rémy, your ear's bleeding.' Using her cardigan sleeve, she dabbed the blood. 'What did you hear?'

Rémy grimaced. 'A piccolo, or maybe a flute at its highest dogs-only pitch.'

Matt shimmied off the roof and dropped in front of them. 'I hate to break up the party,' he said. 'But there's a dead guy on the altar.'

12.

SILENCE OF THE LAMBS

nside the church the apparition had draped itself over everything. The priceless art on the walls, the statues in their alcoves, the computers, desks and shelves of books, all were washed in the strange green light.

Orion's secret HQ was more like a sanctuary for lost or forgotten art than a church: a museum to the sacred and the profane, paintings and sculptures piled high or propped up against one another. Here a modern sculpture of an anvil removed from a museum in Russia because it stirred observers to violence, there a set of Leonardo da Vinci sketches from the estate of an Animare who had recently died. The church was also an art-gallery-slash-supernatural-transit-station where Orion agents travelled from place to place via paintings from artists like Titian and Turner, Van Gogh and Velasquez, Kollwitz and Cassatt. Banksy too. All were secret Animare, men and women like Matt and Em that Orion had been formed to protect.

Rémy, Matt and Em peered anxiously down the aisle.

'It's like we're in that final scene from *The Silence of the Lambs*,' said Em at last. 'You know, in the cellar?'

'Yeah,' said Rémy with a shiver. 'The night-vision goggles.'

'Helloooo, precious,' Matt whispered in Em's ear, making his sister scream.

'You're a dick,' snapped Em when she had recovered.

Matt's eyes were an advantage in the dark. He confidently led the way deeper into the sanctuary, while Em and Rémy collided with work tables and freestanding pews before their eyes adjusted and they could see the outline of the body splayed on the simple stone altar. Here, the spectre was at its most frenetic, rising from the body like a tornado, before spreading out across the ceiling in rushing waves of light.

Matt checked for a pulse. 'Definitely dead.' He crouched and looked more closely, then rocked back on his heels. 'Aw, Em. It's Gibson.'

Em grew even paler in the dim light.

'Who's Gibson?' Rémy asked.

'One of Orion's oldest agents.' Em sounded choked. 'He'd just retired. His arthritis was bad and he had a heart condition. He was active in the Second World War, can you believe that?'

Rémy studied the figure on the altar. Gibson was wearing pyjamas, blue-and-white striped ones buttoned to the top, and a navy dressing gown with big pockets.

His face looked pale and peaceful. His lips were not yet blue.

Matt cleared his throat. 'He doesn't look like he's been injured or attacked.'

'We have to call Vaughn,' said Em, tears filling her eyes. 'He'll tell the people who need to know.'

'We can't,' said Matt. 'He's at the meeting.'

'We'll have to call Mum, then,' Em said. 'Or Grandpa, or Simon.'

'They're *all* at the meeting, Em.'

'What meeting?' Rémy asked, trying to keep up.

'The annual world conference for all the Councils of Guardians,' Matt explained. 'They hang out and discuss Animare like us and Gibson here, moaning about the trouble we cause with our artsy, reality-altering habits. Then they create more bloody rules.'

Rémy waved at the paintings on the walls. 'So why don't we just go find them? You guys can fade us into these pictures and take us anywhere in the world.'

'We don't know where they gather,' Matt confessed. 'They do these things on a need-to-know basis.'

'And we definitely do not need to know,' said Em resentfully.

The air in the room fizzed with static. The lights above Gibson's body were pulsing more quickly and brighter than before.

Em shivered. 'Do you feel that?'

'I feel it,' Matt said.

Matt reached into the pocket of Gibson's dressing gown, placing sweets, a small tube of heartburn pills, a monogrammed hanky and the stubs of four charcoal grey pencils on to the slabs of stone. As he rolled Gibson on to his side, a Moleskine notebook opened at a page full of sketches trapped awkwardly in his hand. Matt carefully extracted the notebook from the agent's gnarly fingers and handed it to Em, who stared at the pages.

'His last sketch is of the Constable portal over there.' She nodded to one of the shadowy paintings in a nearby alcove. 'He must have faded here from the National Gallery in Edinburgh.'

'What if he was having a heart attack,' said Matt, 'and faded here just to be safe?'

'Safe from what?' asked Rémy, a bit anxiously.

'A death animation.' Em fetched a throw from a nearby couch and gently covered Gibson's body with it. 'When a powerful Animare dies, if he's painting or drawing or creating in any way at the moment of his death, his imagination can animate spontaneously.'

'Good to know,' said Rémy, his eyes wide.

Matt waved his hand in the shifting green air. 'It doesn't happen often, but when it does, it can go crazy. Gibson must have left a pretty powerful death animation to produce a massive residual of light like this.'

There was a fierce kick of piercing music that made Rémy catch his breath and reach for his iPod. He turned the control wheel to a playlist of static, and shoved the buds into his ears.

'Whatever this dude created when he died,' Rémy said, screwing up his face, 'it comes with its own soundtrack. And it's getting stronger.'

13.

A CHILDREN'S PARADE

The strange exodus of children from Kentigern began right after sun-up. The light was much less visible as clouds drifted across the morning sky.

Mabel and Ben Lambert were the first to leave, followed by the Denby children. The five were soon seven, and then quickly eight, as more children spewed from houses and headed barefoot towards the main road, skipping past the pitch where the primary school football team was about to begin an early practice. The parade crossed the pitch at the moment the coach had her back to the path, arranging orange cones for a practice drill. When she turned round again, the three boys and two girls, led by her main striker Tommy Scanlon, had joined the end of the snaking line.

The coach blew her whistle. 'Ye wee buggers! Get back here now!'

The children kept marching, following Mabel and Ben along the path. The coach blew her whistle again.

More children were joining them, three darting from the big houses tucked into the hillside, then two more from the flat above the newsagent's.

The coach grabbed her phone from her backpack and dialled 999.

'The weans!' she said urgently. 'Something's happening to them. It's like they've been hypnotized!'

'Have you been drinking, miss?'

Dropping her phone, the coach sprinted along the grass. The children were either going to turn on to the normally busy A14, or up towards the treacherous ruins of St Mungo's Castle. The coach prayed they would take the A14.

A wild-eyed woman joined her. The coach recognized her from the school playground: Collyn Lambert.

'Mabel!' shouted Collyn. 'You and your brother need to stop this nonsense right now!'

But Mabel and Ben were oblivious. They, and the rest of the children, seemed to be focusing on something just beyond their field of vision.

'Mabel!' screamed Collyn piteously. 'Please. Where are you going?'

Bill Preston, the local constable, swerved his Ford Fiesta to a stop on the pavement, lights flashing, sirens screaming. Not even wee emergency-vehicle-obsessed Ben Lambert turned his head as the parade swept round the police car.

Collyn went into full panic mode and launched

herself at her children's legs, but a strange energy field surrounding her children snapped her wrists back and her face crunched up against it as if she'd hit a wall. She howled as she face-planted on the stony road.

Mabel, Ben and the other children climbed over her prostrate body and marched on.

14.

ONWARDS TO THE CASTLE

C ollyn Lambert leaped to her feet, ignoring the bumps and scratches from the children. She was a runner and in minutes managed to sprint well ahead of the children. She stood at the bottom of the steep path up to the castle, turning her eyes to the swirling light whose thin tails stretched all the way back to the old church.

The apparition looked familiar. Collyn's heart jolted and her adrenaline surged.

The children were making their way purposefully along the road to the car park and the entrance to the castle. Collyn snapped herself out of paralysis.

'The bridge!' she screamed to the other pursuing adults. 'We need to stop them before they climb this path to the bridge!'

The castle's stone bridge was striped in shadows from the morning sun. It was wide enough for two adults to cross at the same time while hiking up the rocky pass and into the ruins, but children were not allowed on the bridge without adult supervision. The gully beneath it had once been part of the moat for the castle, and was deep and lined with jagged rocks.

'The turnstile is closed,' gasped Mitch, Tommy Scanlon's dad, jogging up next to Collyn. 'Maybe the barrier will stop them from getting on to the path. It'll slow them down until we think of something, at least.'

'What in God's name is happening to them?' Collyn cried, grabbing Mitch's coat sleeves. 'They look drugged, but all my Mabel ate this mornin' was jammy toast and cereal.'

'Our Tommy left the extra football practice,' said Mitch, shaking his head in disbelief. 'He never leaves football practice.'

'Jesus,' moaned Collyn. 'Look at their feet. They're a' skint.'

The small car park was filled with stunned parents calling to their kids to stop. But the children, bloody feet and all, stomped on. Someone had brought out a long hose and was squeezing the handle. The water simply fanned away and over the children as if a massive umbrella was shielding them.

One by one, the children marched up the hillside to the turnstile at the castle entrance. Those who were too small to climb over it, like Ben, crawled underneath. The pace slowed as a hundred tiny bare feet trudged up the steep hill, but they never stopped moving.

'We have to think of something,' pleaded Mitch, staring into the gully.

Collyn gazed, transfixed, at the entrance to the castle ruins where the phantasm was fully manifesting itself. Like a figure from a Dali painting, a surreal, elongated thing was stepping out of the light, through the arched entrance and on to the bridge. With every weightless step, the bells jingled on its cuffs and jangled on the curled toes of his boots. The figure was androgynous, with rubbery limbs completely out of proportion with its torso. It was dressed in purple tunic and gold leggings. It had no face, no eyes and no nose. Only its red lips had any solid presence, blowing into a piccolo, as its foot in its curled boot *tap, tap, tap*ped rhythmically on the arched stone.

'What in the name of… What is that?' stuttered Mitch, mopping his brow with the back of his hand.

Collyn found her voice. 'It's a piper,' she said. 'A Pied Piper.'

15.

SHELF LIFE

'If this phantom is from a death animation,' said Rémy, staring up at the glowing cloud seeping through the ceiling of the church, 'won't it just disappear on its own after Gibson's been dead for a while?'

'It will,' said Matt as they headed outside again, 'but the problem is, there's no predicting the shelf life. Could be an hour. Could be a day. Might be weeks.'

'And it might have done a lot of damage by then,' added Em.

'So what do you – *we* – do?'

'It would help if we knew what Gibson was working on before he died,' Em said. 'But since it would take ages to figure that out, I guess we follow the spectre and see where it's ended up.'

'From what I could see, it looked as if it was gathering itself in the castle ruins,' said Matt, 'which means it's likely been spotted.'

Em took out her sketchpad. 'I'll draw us something to get us to the castle more quickly.'

Rémy watched as her fingertips etched lines of light and colour across the page. The way the twins brought their art to life awed him every time he saw it.

Suddenly, the church door began to throb, as if something or someone was trapped inside and struggling to escape. Then, just when it looked as if it was imploding, a ball of silver light enveloped the entrance to the church.

'Em, are you kidding me?' Matt breathed.

'Now that's *lit*!' said Rémy as he backed away.

'I'm trying to minimize our carbon footprint,' said Em, rubbing her hand along the candelabra of antlers on the white peryton in front of them. The beast snorted and bowed its massive head and muscular front legs at Em's touch.

'There's room for all of us,' said Matt, scrambling on to the creature's broad back and helping Em on behind him.

Rémy climbed up awkwardly, wrapping his arms round Em's waist. 'If my mom could see me now,' he muttered as the peryton tossed its head and broke into a gallop. 'She freaked when I rode my bike to school.'

16.

NOTHING BUT NET

The Pied Piper's faceless head bobbed to the rhythm of his playing as his tune changed from a march to a playful jig. The aura of light surrounding him was pulsing to the faster beat, most of it in a glowing cloud of green light anchored above the castle. The car park was packed, tensions were high, and adrenaline was pumping in gallons through the crowd.

'What about a net?' yelled Billy Preston, his radio crackling on his uniformed shoulder.

'Where in hell would we get a net?' Jimmy McDonald yelled back. His five-year-old daughter, Fiona, was in the middle of the march.

'Don't be an arsehole, Jimmy, Ah'm only trying to help. It's more than yer doing.'

Jimmy leaped over his wife, who was on her knees in prayer, and punched the constable square in the chest. The fight might have easily erupted into a brawl if Collyn Lambert hadn't interrupted.

'The kids are on the bridge!' she screamed.

Alice Schaefer and Marcia Buckingham dropped to their knees next to Shona McDonald while Jimmy and Billy scrambled up off the ground, wiping blood from their noses.

Mabel stepped first on to the bridge. Ben, Tommy, Fiona and all the other children followed. The adults held their collective breath.

'It's OK. It's OK. Step steady, Mabel. You can do it, my love, you can do it,' whispered Collyn, wringing her hands at the sight of her daughter's uncertain steps.

Mabel was almost at the middle of the bridge when her foot slipped. Gravel crumbled from the edge and rained into the gully. She slid on to her bottom. Collyn gasped, digging her nails into her palms.

Ben toddled out to help his big sister. Slowly Mabel got up, but she was wobbling close to the edge and Ben's hold on her was making her balance worse. She kept one hand on Ben's shirt while she tried to steady herself on the iron chain, the only barrier between her tiny body and the treacherous drop. But Ben was crying now and Mabel put too much weight on the chain. Lost her footing.

Both children swung out over the crevasse.

The screams from the car park hit Rémy like brain-freeze. He gasped and tightened his grip on Em, who squeezed his hand comfortingly on her waist.

The peryton soared in a tight circle above the castle, its wings creating a draught of air that bent the tree-tops and created a swirl of silver fog that kept them invisible to the crowd. The rush of air made it difficult for the three of them to hear each other, even the twins' ability to talk to each other telepathically was muted this close to the death animation.

The peryton banked lower. Em sketched desperately with her free hand while below them, one by one, Mabel, Ben and all the other young children toppled from the bridge and into the abyss.

17.

NEITHER HERE NOR THERE

Ah, such fools are madmen and martyrs, thought Caravaggio, stepping out of a dark, painted corner of *The Calling of St Matthew.* He took a moment to admire his own genius in the brushwork and then, leaning over the figure of the tax collector in the middle of the canvas, set a fan of playing cards face-up on his lap.

With loud sighs, the other figures in the painting folded their cards. St Peter snorted and turned away. Jesus rolled his eyes.

'Why is it that your hand always wins, Caravaggio?' complained the tax collector.

'Because, my noble friend, I cheat.' Caravaggio bowed low to the five figures seated round the table.

Reaching beneath his white tunic, he freed his sketch-pad from his leather waistband. He spat three times on the wedge of charcoal he'd trapped between the pages and began to sketch his way out of his painted space into the real world.

With speed and skill, he ran the charcoal across the paper, first outlining the figures at the table before filling in details of arms and legs, a pointing finger, an open window. Without pausing, he shaded furiously until the background of the painting shimmered with waves of light and the foreground melted around him. The wall and the window dissolved in thick trails of paint, oozing like tar over the figures poised round the table, each one liquefying into the other until the painting looked as if someone had wiped oil over the canvas.

Caravaggio's fingers flashed over the sketch like feathery quills of light until he began to separate from his art. First, his arms came through the massive canvas, outstretched like a mummy rising from its tomb. His muscular torso, shoulders and head followed fast, as if some invisible presence was expelling him from the painting. Every part of him was covered in a spectral membrane as he faded from his art into reality.

Caravaggio held himself still in that stretched position for a moment, the caul tethering him to his creation. For one beautiful, orgasmic instant, he lingered between these two realities. *This must be what divine rapture is like,* he thought. Souls caught neither here nor there, in a moment neither now nor then.

When he finally collapsed on to the cold marble floor of the Church of San Luigi dei Francesi in Rome, his bones ached and his eyes were bleeding, but he was laughing. What a rush of ideas and emotions he experienced after such a charged moment. If only he was in his studio surrounded by his paint pots and inks, what images he would create.

His skin reeked of linseed oil and his tongue was thick with yellow pigment. He sat for a few more seconds in the side chapel and combed his fingers through his long dark curls, shaking out flakes of paint that danced like dust in the moonlight piercing a stained-glass window nearby.

His knees cracked as he stood up. At least it wasn't his head this time. He winced at the memory. Ten years earlier, when he'd first faded from *The Calling of St Matthew*, he had landed head first on the marble steps in front of the small altar. The injury had knocked all sense from him, leaving him bewildered, and with a blinding headache. He recalled staunching the bleeding above his eye with an unfamiliar monogrammed kerchief, and wobbling to his feet when he heard two loud clicks and a long whir.

The tiny chapel had lit up as bright as the sun, and a group of people dressed the likes of which he'd never seen in his life gawked at him.

A woman had screamed, 'He's going to vandalize the paintings!' over and over again. Her words were unfamiliar, but their tone, brash and threatening, was unfortunately not.

Two men had reached over the rope barrier in an attempt to grab him. Confused and bleeding, Caravaggio had scrambled under the rope and hidden in a cordoned-off section of the church. And when he regained his senses, he was aware of two startling factors: it was no longer 1610, and, despite the gash above his eye, he was no longer dying.

Since that terrifying afternoon, he had returned regularly to these paintings, hoping that the broad strokes of what had happened the day he fell into the future would be clearer. But even after ten years of reading everything he could find about himself – biographies, academic papers, exhibit catalogues, even novels, which he decided often held the most truth about his life – the events surrounding his so-called death remained fragmented and fleeting. Soldiers swarming a palazzo, flames devouring a bedchamber, swarming rats on a murky river, a twisting pain in his side, and then nothing until his head had hit that marble floor.

A skittering noise beneath the nearby pews brought his mind back to the present. Rats scavenging for food. Some things never changed, no matter how much time passed. He sat on the steps, recovering his equilibrium from his dramatic fade, and gazed at the three paintings on the walls around him. *The Calling of St Matthew*, *The Martyrdom of St Matthew* and *The Inspiration of St Matthew* had been commissions for Cardinal Borghese. Or was it Barbarini? Caravaggio shook his head, sending puffs of yellow into the air. He could no longer remember that detail either.

The Calling faced *The Martyrdom*, in which Matthew's killer stood naked with his arm about to strike while a cherubic angel floated in a soft cloud about the saint, offering him his hand. The commission had made his name in Rome in his own time, but Caravaggio knew from his research that he wasn't credited as revolutionary for another two hundred years. Eighteenth-century academics described him as 'an artist virtuous in his play of light and dark and groundbreaking in his representation of the divine in the ordinary'.

He ran his hands through his long dark hair and smirked. He may have been in demand in the sixteenth, studied in the eighteenth and acclaimed in the twenty-first centuries, but virtuous he was not ... in any time.

18.

THIS PLACE IS LIT

Climbing over the low wall that separated the side chapel from the church's historic nave, Caravaggio withdrew his dagger and used its blade to crack open the same black light box that had startled him after that first fall a decade ago. He had since noted with interest how tourists dropped coins inside to illuminate his triptych for two minutes. In the ten years since his resurrection, this box was one of his regular sources of income.

He counted out enough coins to feed, house and clothe him for the next few days. More than ever before, he needed to blend in. Two weeks earlier, he'd sworn to Orion on his honour to remain hidden, no matter what.

He'd kept his word. Almost.

Dropping the money into the leather pouch tied to his belt, he took a few steps into the aisle – and stopped. Something was wrong. The air was suddenly cold.

The colossal pipe organ heaved a breath and released a gust of air that chased the flames from all the candles and knocked the massive gold-encrusted candelabra from the main altar. Terror froze Caravaggio where he stood. The air was heavy with gunpowder and sulphur, and he dropped to his knees, a sharp pain piercing his temple. He clenched his jaw and bit his tongue and cried out, a shard of a memory filling his throat and squeezing his heart. These were the smells of a long-forgotten bedchamber.

All around him, ancient bones snapped in every sarcophagus and buried coffin in the church. A fissure exploded from beneath the main altar and snaked down the nave and aisles, splitting open the marble floor. Skeletal hands, headless necks and broken shoulders rose through the ruptures like diabolical weeds. In seconds, the floor was littered with body parts. The stench was overpowering. Caravaggio grabbed the threadbare mono-grammed kerchief he still carried and held it to his face.

The organ heaved again, a wailing chord like a choir of angry beasts. The artist threw himself to the ground as every piece of glass in the church, from stained-glass windows to the leaded glass on the reliquary of a long-forgotten pope, exploded in a million pieces.

Frantically, he brushed shards from his face and hands. The pain in his temple was a fork of lightning, sending agony and a piercing white-hot pain to every limb. He squeezed his eyes closed against a tornado of images: a dark shapeless being ascending from a sea of stunning colours, enfolded in black wings, heads and mouths suckling at its breasts. The organ belted out another screaming chord. Caravaggio collapsed to the floor, vomiting bile.

The air in the side chapel ticked once, twice, three times, like a fire struggling to light. Slowly, the artist turned and stared in terror at *The Martyrdom*. At St Matthew squirming beneath the foot of his naked killer.

Only it wasn't St Matthew any more.

Caravaggio cringed at the sight of his own face drawn in agony beneath the killer's blade. Above his head, the cloud of pure white opened like a gaping mouth and swallowed the cherub. From the centre of the canvas flowed a white ethereal mist, with a stench of phosphorous that hit the artist like a punch to his gut. His insides twisted in knots. The pain in his head numbed his thoughts, leaving him drenched in fear and gasping from the feeling that this blasphemy manifesting in his art was a result of his own actions.

The organ exhaled again, a frenzied, unholy sound. Bones twitched, clicking against the marble like wind-up toys. Skulls cracked in half, their smiles splitting their jaws. The diabolical music flooded the nave. Caravaggio pressed his hands to his ears, dragging himself further into the shadows, pressing his back against the wall beneath the light box. Suddenly the organ breathed a low sigh and was silent.

And something deep inside *The Martyrdom* coughed.

Caravaggio had seen and heard enough. He felt his way unsteadily along the wall towards the grand wooden doors at the entrance, crunching on the bones of popes and cardinals and shattering them underfoot. But then he stopped, one hand on the door. He could not help himself. Like Orpheus in the Underworld, longing for one last sight of his love, Eurydice, he looked back.

The side chapel was bathed in a silver-grey light as a thunderous cloud stretched from the centre of *The Martyrdom* to the heart of *The Calling*, connecting the paintings in a heaving mass. The cloud was trembling. Alive. Bolts of light shot to its core from each of the canvases. The bolts coiled together like lovers, forming a brilliant fireball out of which a magnificent, perfectly formed figure emerged. Head bowed in supplication, muscular arms folded in front of its genitals, long blond curls covering its face, every part of its body pulsed with power.

Caravaggio gazed in terrified awe as the figure lifted its arms, rivulets of light dripping from its long elegant fingers. From its back, thick, black, silver-tipped wings slowly unfolded, as wide as the side chapel itself. The divine creature raised its head and stared directly at him.

A series of images crashed through Caravaggio's mind. A canvas wrapped in a bolt of cloth. A carriage fleeing over a hillside. A peach, ripe and rotten.

He yanked open the doors of the church and ran for his life.

Again.

19.

THE CIRCUS
CAME TO TOWN

The majestic peryton dipped gracefully into the rocky hollow beneath the stone bridge, keeping Matt, Em and Rémy shrouded in its animated haze.

With the screams of parents still echoing around the castle, the village children squealed as if the circus had come to town, bringing a bouncy house with it. Where they should have fallen on the wicked rocks far below the bridge, they were playing on a bed of soft multi-coloured balls with which Em had filled the gully, falling and laughing over each other, their squeals of delight in stark contrast to the anguished howls of their parents moments earlier.

'Put me down on the bridge,' said Rémy. 'I can take care of the Piper.'

'Sure?' said Matt. 'This is new territory for you. I can handle him without any trouble.'

'Just do it.' Rémy's nerves were frayed enough, given the circumstances. Did Matt really have to question his abilities too?

Em leaned forward and whispered into the peryton's ear. The beast swooped up and circled above the Pied Piper, who played on as if it was still on the page of whatever story Gibson had been illustrating or reading when he died.

Rémy swung his leg round and dropped from the considerable height on to the bridge. His knees buckled as he slammed against the stones, but then he found his balance fast and faced the Piper.

'Let's see what you're made of, fool,' he said.

Rémy slipped his harmonica from his pocket and began to play. Starting slow, with an achingly sombre blues riff, he let the soft, slurred notes quieten his mind, shutting out the chaos around him and the mythical beast above. The Piper rocked on to its toes and played faster, its mouth stretching into a crazed grin.

'Dude, you ain't gonna win this one.'

After three more long notes, Rémy tilted his head, cupped his harmonica tighter, and blew into an Irish jig that matched the trilling sounds of the Piper's piccolo.

The Piper cocked its head as Rémy's notes crashed into it. Its lips puckered, its head flipped side to side like a robot with its circuits scrambled. Rémy played a loud bending note of the first verse. The Piper's jingling, pointed feet disappeared. Rémy played the chorus.

The Piper's body stretched higher and higher above the bridge until it came close to slamming into the hooves of the peryton. Rémy repeated the chorus until he no longer saw the bridge, the Piper or the peryton: just his music weaving like silver ribbons among the green lines of the animation. He was Neo seeing the Matrix, or the Sandman shaping forms. He was Rémy Dupree Rush, a Conjuror.

He hit a high C. The Piper swelled to three times his girth and then exploded, leaving Rémy in gobs of paint and stinking of rotten eggs.

20.

ALL THE
HAPPY ZOMBIES

Rémy stepped out of the shower and dried off quickly. The tower bathroom was the size of a telephone box. Em had her own en-suite, but Rémy and Matt shared this one. He shivered as he pulled on fresh jeans and a T-shirt. He could still smell the turpentine on his skin.

'Still a bit gamey in there?' said Matt through the shower-room door. 'Happens to the best of us.'

'You could have warned me the animation would explode,' Rémy retorted.

Matt's laughter rang in his words. 'Yeah, but where's the fun in that?'

Em cut in. 'Thought you'd want to know we inspirited everyone, then led all the happy zombies home.'

'Any of the kids hurt?'

'Nah,' said Matt. 'A few cuts and scrapes.'

'We did manage to get through to Vaughn via back

channels,' said Em. 'He'll notify Gibson's family. He just asked us to take the body to Orion's undertaker in Edinburgh.'

'Do you need help?' asked Rémy, sitting on the edge of the toilet and pulling on his unlaced boots.

'All done,' said Matt. 'Fading with a dead body's definitely weird, but we managed. We didn't need any of your musical accompaniment for this one.'

Rémy didn't add anything, his anger at Matt stewing beneath his skin.

'Rémy,' said Em. 'Thanks for your help this morning. Sorry again about the gross splatter.'

Rémy waited until he heard Matt and Em's footsteps disappear up to the top of the tower before he opened the door. At least Em had apologized, which was more than could be said for her brother. Plus she had sent him home on the peryton, while she and Matt had remained in the castle parking lot.

Instead of returning to his room, Rémy slouched down the tower stairs and into the church. He stopped in the scullery to shove his paint-covered clothes into the washing machine before heading to the kitchen, where he microwaved a mug of chicken broth and carried it into the nave.

Everything that had happened to him in the past few months was still so unreal. The Camarilla's attempt to kill him had failed, but their forces were legion and they were not about to give up. His conjuring powers were necessary to stop the rise of their prophesied Second Kingdom, a hell on earth with humanity enslaved.

It seemed an age ago instead of only months since he'd fled Chicago after the brutal death of his mother and his beloved Tía Rosa. 'Find the Moor,' his mother had whispered with her dying breath. And he had. Or rather, the Moor had found him. But even with Orion's help, too many of his mother's secrets remained. Too much still needed to be learned. Rémy sometimes wondered if the Camarilla's Second Kingdom wasn't already here.

He kneeled over a grate on the stone floor and pried it open. He leaned into the space, lifted out a lockbox, and carried it to the table where he unlocked it with the key his mom had given him right before she died. He settled at the table tucked in the shadows of one of the small chapels, and studied everything that she had left him.

Annie Dupree Rush's journal was no longer bulging with loose pages, as it had been when Rémy had found it. Her sketches, torn images from gallery catalogues, leaves of sheet music and random pages of text copied from documents and manuscripts concerning her research on the Second Kingdom had all been cata-logued and preserved in Orion's database. He traced his fingers over his mom's scribbled loopy handwriting in her journal.

Watchers: primordial. Rebel angels? Demons? Both? Their offspring?

The journal had also been digitized, but Rémy refused to work from the copy. His mom's voice sang from every page. He wasn't ready to hear silence.

From the scullery, the washing machine rocked against the stone floor, the radiators hissed, and the paintings bellowed at Rémy in dissonant notes and pitchy chords. But he could hear something else too: a bass line throbbing beneath the rest. Residual from Gibson's death, perhaps.

Untangling his headphones from his pocket, he clicked his playlist of static from his old iPod. The white noise might counteract the cacophony that was setting his mind on edge and interfering with his concentration. The droning continued to disturb him. He looked over at the altar again. Nothing ... and yet there was *something* competing for his attention.

Rémy untied the lace fastening the journal and opened to the page he'd been working on earlier in the day. His mother had traced one of the earliest historical mentions of the Second Kingdom to the *Book of Songs*, a manuscript written by a favourite at the court of the Roman Emperor Hadrian. Rémy gulped the rest of his soup as he studied the page, thinking about his mother's love of ancient history, a passion that had consumed her almost as much as her love of music and ... and of him.

Frustrated, sad and tired, he pushed the journal to one side and gazed at the whiteboard showing his family tree. A locket portrait of Rémy's ancestor, Alfonso Blue, an overseer of the Dupree plantation in Louisiana, was held with a magnet at the top of the tree, and a wedding photograph of his parents – the father he never knew and the mother he wished he'd known better – at the vast Dupree mansion, was at the centre. A more recent photograph of his mother sitting at her roll-top desk, its legs carved to look like sugarcane leaves and its rows of rectangular cubbies bulging with her correspondence, was pinned beneath.

Something about the second picture of his mother snagged Rémy's curiosity. But it was impossible to concentrate on account of the noise. It was coming from outside, he realized, and was a higher pitch than before, less like a droning human and more like a wailing cat.

Quickly, Rémy tucked the journal back inside the lockbox, returned it to the space beneath the floor and dropped the grate. He pulled out his headphones and stepped out into the cool Highland air. The crying was not loud enough to draw anyone else's attention, but he knew it was calling for his. The mark of the Conjuror beneath his hairline at the back of his neck started pulsing, a trembling that made him shiver.

The sound was coming from the cemetery on the cap of the hill behind the church.

21.

PERSECUTED
AND BANISHED

Rémy headed for the graveyard in the moonlight, jogging his way up the hill through the pine trees and the brambles until he reached the first row of headstones. He read them. They were from the seventeenth and eighteenth centuries from the looks of it. He used the toe of his boot to scrape off the moss and read the first inscription:

PERSECUTED AND BANISHED
SUFFERED BUT SURVIVED
1694–1715

Suffered but survived. Story of his life. His whole family's, come to think of it. The words made him think about his mom and her grave. He didn't even know where her body had ended up.

The hill grew steeper the closer Rémy got to the monument at the heart of the cemetery: a sandstone statue of a Highland soldier leaning slightly forward on a walking stick with a peryton at its head. The soldier was in Highland dress with a sweeping wrap tossed over his shoulder. Part of his sporran had come away, and his right foot was broken off at the ankle. The soldier was standing on a three-tiered circular pedestal, giving him a spectacular view of the Scottish countryside. Rémy climbed on to the second tier before pausing for breath.

He looked out across the tapestry of the countryside, noting the church of Orion and its tower snuggled under the lip of the hill, the spotlights on the ruins of St Mungo's Castle and the soft glow of porch lights from the village off in the distance. Most of the village windows were dark, its inhabitants none the worse for the terror earlier in the day. The air was fragrant with fresh mint and damp cut grass. This time in early fall, from the balcony outside his mom's bedroom, the air smelled of KFC, exhaust fumes, cigarettes and smoke from neighbourhood grills. His mom would have liked it here.

A wave of homesickness hit Rémy so hard that he lost his balance and steadied himself on the monument. The moment his palms pressed on the carved marble, the wailing sound blasted inside his head, dizzying his thoughts further. He closed his eyes, trying to force the sound to take shape, to slow down, to let him see what was so urgent, but the fragments were gone before he could make sense of them. All that lingered in his head was a chord progression from the beginning of a song that Rémy couldn't quite place. He hummed the chords – but got nothing.

The Conjuror's mark burned insistently, firing pain up his neck. The entire monument was keening. He took two steps away and slipped his harmonica from his back pocket. Conjuring might summon the twins, but he decided he didn't care. Whatever was calling to him from within this monument was worth disturbing their sleep.

Wiping his harmonica on his thigh, he held it to his lips, his hands cupped loosely around it, his fingers pointed slightly in the air. He blew a long warm-up note into the mouthpiece. Played double notes, using his tongue to layer the sound as he built to a crescendo that he held for a long note, sweat dripping into his eyes, his fingers a blur in the music.

Before him the front of the pedestal came crumbling down.

22.

IMPOSSIBLE
TO RESIST

Stone dust danced a furious jig in the moonlight, settling over Rémy and the statue of the Highlander like a flurry of snow. The monument looked as if a jackhammer had crushed the front of it, leaving an opening that invited Rémy to step inside.

For a moment, Rémy was too breathless to move. He dropped to the ground until his vision cleared and his hands felt firmly attached to his wrists again. He rolled his neck, stretching his muscles, conscious of the mark pulsing on his neck. When he felt in control again, he crawled into the hole.

The wailing sounded softer here, like a child crying. There was a narrow wooden door in the grip of serious cobwebs and thick black dust shone in a ribbon of moonlight. He rubbed the grime between his fingers. Charcoal. Interesting. The kind Em used to animate. It looked like a blowtorch had melted the door's massive brass lock into a formless mass. Conjuring a key wouldn't do any good. The door's hinges also looked as if they'd been melted.

The droning cried on, touching his skin, electrifying him. He had to know what lay inside this place. He'd faced worse enough already, he reasoned with himself. He had held his murdered mother like a child in his arms as she breathed her last. That was the worst thing of all.

Rémy crawled back outside for a moment, sprinting and sliding down the other side of the hill to a wood-pile where he and Matt had been breaking up dead trees for the church's wood burner. Before grabbing the axe, he looked across at the church tower. Candle-light flickered from Em's room at the top. She was still awake. Matt's window was dark, but given Matt's issues with his eyes, that didn't necessarily mean he was asleep.

The urgency Rémy felt was impossible to resist. He scrambled back up the hill and swung the axe into the wood panel above the lock. The wood cracked easily, but the smashed lock held firm. Rémy ran his charcoal-stained fingers over the melted metal, wondering if a long time ago an Animare had sealed this chamber.

He swung the axe again and again until he'd torn a wide gash in the wood. Then he reached his hand through to try the lock on the other side. Something skittered over his fingers and he jerked his hand back. Rats.

The noise moaned through the gaping hole, bringing with it a breath of putrid air. Rémy kept hacking until the lock hung like a rotten tooth from a mouth of darkness. Then he climbed through.

23.

AMONG THE DEAD

A set of stone steps plummeted into darkness, an iron gate blocking the way. Rémy gave it a shove. It was rusty and swung open easily.

Cautiously, he stepped forward, pressing his hands flat against the walls on each side. He made it down the first three steps, but four and five crumbled, knocking him to his knees so that he tumbled and smacked his head.

He sat up against the wall, gingerly touching the side of his head. No blood, but he was going to have a nasty bump. *Should have grabbed a torch from the scullery,* he thought, but he wasn't going back to grab one now.

When they'd first arrived at Orion, Em had given Rémy a tour. She'd explained how the church had been a sanctuary for Covenanters, Scottish revolutionaries, in the sixteenth century. Rémy wondered if these steps led to an underground safe house.

The darkness was damp, suffocating. The wailing was louder, a keening lament making his heart race and his anxiety rise. He sat on the steps and took out his harmonica again, warming up quickly with a progression of chords. Then he slipped into a bright melody, and before he slurred his last note, a camping lantern dropped out of a swirl of haze to land on his lap.

The steps turned in a steep right angle only a few metres in front of him: a turn where he'd have hit a lot harder if he hadn't fallen where he did. He kept descending with a turn every three or four steps until the wailing sounded as if it was seeping through the walls on both sides of him. The dampness was worse the deeper he went, webs of moss creeping through the cracks on the stone, making the steps even more treacherous.

Finally, Rémy hit a dead end, catching himself before he crashed into it. He was a long way beneath the pedestal. Sixty-seven steps, in fact. The space was only one or two metres wider than Rémy's outstretched arms, and on his toes he could touch the ceiling. The wailing and the pulsing of the mark were starting to set his teeth on edge, and he was thinking about getting help when the wailing evolved into the chord progression he'd heard earlier.

He hummed the chords over again.

After listening to the riff for a few minutes, Rémy mimicked it on his harmonica. Nothing happened. He played the riff again. Still nothing. But on the final note, the third time, a white light like the flame on a fuse raced down the rock wall, fizzing to a shower of sparks when it reached the ground. That's when the entire wall shifted, opening along the white-hot seam. A gust of stinking air escaped through the opening.

Gripping his harmonica, Rémy stepped into a burial chamber right out of a horror movie, complete with a crumbling effigy on top of a stone tomb and a wall covered with a threadbare tapestry depicting Roman gladiators battling mythical flying beasts. A row of whisky barrels layered with shards of broken pottery stood behind the tomb, and there was what looked like an animal carcass nailed on the wall.

A heavy hand fell on to his shoulder. Rémy freaked, twisted away and dropped the lantern. Everything was plunged into darkness. For the first time that night, he felt his courage wane. His hands were shaking as he fumbled for the lantern and relit it with a soft and trembling breath on his harmonica. A rusting coat of arms was standing near the opening. Rémy snorted at the arm that had dropped when he'd stepped into the chamber. If the wailing hadn't been crippling his brain, Rémy would have laughed. Instead, he set the lantern at his feet and stared up at where a set of rotting bagpipes hung from the wall like a hunting trophy, softly moaning at him.

Directly beneath the bagpipes stretched the resident of the tomb's effigy with a brass coat of arms set into its side. Rémy pulled his sleeve over his hands and rubbed the brass until the inscription was clear.

HERE LIES A' THAT'S MORTAL OF THE HIGHLAND FOX
MASON RENARD CALDER, DUKE OF ALBION
1580–1639

24.

GIVE THEM A WHURL

The call of the pipes was undeniable.

Rémy had never played an instrument like this, but the desire he felt in his bones was all-consuming. The bag was made of hide that he needed to fill with air, but it was stinking and rotten, the skin pocked with holes and an abandoned rodent's nest complete with a bloated carcass inside. He lifted down the wooden pipe, the chanter, instead. It was made of black wood and looked like a recorder but older, much older, with its finger holes rubbed down, smooth to the touch, and an etched silver ring like a collar on the lower neck of the pipe. Without a conscious thought, he put the chanter to his lips and began to play. He began with a long mournful wail, surprised that he'd drawn any sound from the ancient instrument at all. Shutting out his surroundings, he let the music calm his restlessness. He started with *Onward Christian Soldiers*, a favourite of his Tía Rosa's, then *Amazing Grace,* because what else do you play on a chanter?

A gust of air brushed the top of his head, the scent of oranges lingering in its wake. The mark on his neck felt alive under his skin. He played on, faster and louder. He couldn't stop even if he wanted to. The music was wrapping him in a welcoming warmth he hadn't felt in months.

25.

MUST BE A RULE

Em let her nightgown slip off her shoulders. Zach's fingers danced across her freckled skin, sketching an imaginary line down her back. She shivered, a soft moan escaping her lips. The canvas she'd just hung on the wall in front of her was pulsing with light, its beat matching her quickening heart. Her heart broke every time she thought of Zach sending her present back. He didn't want it. He didn't want her.

Her animated-Zach's hair was longer and lighter than before, his hands ink-stained and more calloused. He set them on her hips and smiled down at her before easing her body against his. Their lips brushed, sparks of blue and grey shooting from their touch. Zach narrowed his eyes, crinkling his nose in a way that made her toes tingle.

She led him to her bed where they stretched out, facing each other. She pressed her forehead on to his muscular chest. Oh, how she missed his presence in her life. How the hell had she ended up in this shoebox bedroom in a church tower, like the Lady of Shalott watching the world she'd known drift past?

Zach tilted her chin and kissed her again with an intensity of emotion that brought tears to Em's eyes. It was a kiss that carried the trust of their childhood, the promises of their youth, and the betrayals of their young adulthood. How could the passion still reach her so intensely?

Em knew that what she was doing was seriously frowned upon, but she had missed Zach so much. Besides, she was in the privacy of her own room. Was she shocking the church ghosts? She doubted it. Centuries of feelings had seeped into the cracked stone of the church to such an extent that in the still of the moonlit Highland nights when she was least in control, when her sensitive Guardian nature was at its most vulnerable, she felt all of those passions wash over her.

Zach silently swept Em's short dark hair from her face, twirling strands of her pink streak around his long pale fingers. She sighed and let his touch comfort her, then rolled on to her back and guided his kisses from her lips to her neck. As his tongue touched the soft skin beneath her collarbone, a bolt of desire coursed through every part of her body.

Why had she thrown all this away?

The door to her cell flew open.

'Didn't you hear me?' Matt demanded. 'I've been…' He stopped, wrinkled his nose. 'Oh, for God's sake Em, get a room.'

'I am in a room,' Em protested. 'Mine!'

She scrambled to her sketchpad and tore up the copy of the portrait hanging back on her wall. In a shower of blues and greys, Zach ruptured into a million pieces, splattering Matt and Em with thick drops of acrylic paint.

'Jeezus,' Matt said, grabbing a towel from the sink next to Em's bed.

'What do you want?' said Em, lacing up her boots.

'Rémy's gone,' said Matt.

Em slumped back on to the single bed and rubbed her eyes. With telepathic abilities since birth, she and Matt were way past embarrassing each other with their imaginations. But she was suddenly exhausted at the realization of how much she missed Zach – his wit, his love, and, yes, his body. Much more than she'd been willing to admit.

'What do you mean "gone"?'

Matt spread his hands. 'His bed's empty and I can hear music from the cemetery. Which can't be good.'

Em let her brother pull her up off the bed. She felt his concern ripple through her.

'You'll both be OK,' Matt said gently. 'According to Mum, Zach's loving his internship at MOMA in New York. He's becoming quite the Yankee.'

'That does not make me feel better,' said Em, pulling on her cardigan before trying to slap Matt's head.

He read her intention and ducked. 'I'm pretty sure there's a rule against what you were doing,' he commented, smiling as they jogged down the narrow spiral steps of the church tower.

'I'm pretty sure I don't care.'

26.

THE MARTYRS' MONUMENT

The bagpipe music hit Matt and Em in a visible gust of cold air. It smelled of oranges.

'He's near the Martyrs' Monument,' said Em at once. 'I can feel his longing.'

She took a notebook from her sweater pocket and dashed into the woods.

In seconds Matt was ahead of her, pulling back branches, making their way easier. At the top of the hill in front of the cemetery, he slowed, holding his hand in the air.

'What is it?' Em gasped, resting her hands on her knees.

On the crumbling wall near the churchyard gate, an English soldier in a bloodied redcoat and a tattered powdered wig sat up on his haunches. Strips of pink flesh hung from his forehead like a cap and his eye sockets crawled with maggots. The right side of his face was resting in his shoulder, hanging from his head by ribbons of ropey black tendons. Black gunpowder burns tattooed his neck and chest. His lower jaw clicked rhythmically against his gold epaulettes but nothing, not a growl, was emanating from him.

The only sound was the rush of the wind in the trees and the quickening tune from the bagpipes. A swirling blue haze carpeted the cemetery, rising and falling in peaks and valleys alongside the music. Behind the soldier, a woman dressed in a ball gown pirouetted in front of a grave. It was like the last dance at a zombie ceilidh.

'By all that's holy,' breathed Matt. 'The bawheid's conjured up the dead.'

Em made to run into the churchyard, but Matt held her back. 'Wait,' he said.

'What's your plan?' Em demanded.

'You distract the zombies and I'll stop Rémy.'

'That's not—'

But Matt was already running to the monument, where the music was louder, the wind warmer and the scent of oranges off the charts. Em followed. Her and zombies: not happening. Perhaps if they stopped Rémy's playing, the dead would vanish by themselves.

But Rémy was not so easy to find. The demented redcoat turned from the gate, spotted the two teenagers, rose and charged. He caught Matt first and took him down, jaws snapping together, biting his cheek. Frantically Matt scrambled on the ground for a tree branch or at least a stick. Finding a big rock instead, he smacked it on the soldier's head. The soldier's grip loosened long enough for Matt to roll free.

Em was sketching furiously. 'Use this!' she yelled.

Matt caught the tranquillizer gun as it unfurled in a ribbon of yellow in the space in front of him. He fired, hitting the soldier in what remained of his chest. The red-coat dropped to his tattered knees, tried to rise again, and then flopped flat on the ground, soaking away into the soil like a scarlet ink blot.

'The music's stopped,' said Em suddenly.

The twirling girl in the ball gown vanished as a tall figure crawled from the centre of the Martyrs' Monument and dusted down his T-shirt.

Matt lunged, knocking Rémy back against two grave-stones that toppled under their weight. 'You could have killed us!' he roared. 'You and your walking dead…'

'You and your superior artsy shit…' Rémy yelled back.

'Stop it,' yelled Em. 'Both of you!'

Matt rolled away from Rémy, but Rémy wasn't letting him off so easily. He grabbed a branch and swung it at Matt's stomach. As Matt cut to the left, the branch tore at his jacket. Glancing at the rip across his pocket, he gasped and leaped at Rémy in fury, sending him crashing against the side of the monument and winding him.

Rémy was twisting handfuls of Matt's hair and Matt was punching at the flesh under Rémy's chin when Em shot both of them with darts from the tranquillizer gun.

27.

THE GREAT
WHITE DUKE

'I can't believe you shot us. My leg's still numb.'

Em banged the freezer shut. She tossed a packet of frozen peas to Matt, who set it against his cheek where Rémy had landed a punch, and another bag of frozen carrots to Rémy, who draped them on his shoulder where Matt had kicked him. Rémy growled. Matt snarled. The cracked Formica table felt like an unstable barrier between them.

'You boys will play nice or else,' Em scowled, sending a frisson of electricity across their scalps.

'He started it,' they both said, pointing to each other almost in unison.

'What are you? Ten?' Em demanded. 'We're trying to stop an apocalypse coming, and you two are trying out for WWE.'

Matt started to speak. Em silenced him with a glare. 'We're all on edge and out of our league, but we have *powers*,' she said. 'And those powers come with responsibility. We use them with purpose.'

'But—' Rémy tried to jump in. Em leaned across the table and squeezed the carrots against his shoulder till he squirmed.

'You're lucky that we're the only ones here tonight,' she hissed at her brother. 'We're supposed to be hiding out, lying low, being invisible to the world until the mess we left in Spain gets sorted. And *you*' – she pointed directly to Rémy – 'I get that you've been thrown into this world without preamble or preparation, but we need you to pull it together or we'll never stop the Camarilla and their Second Coming.'

'Kingdom,' mumbled Rémy.

'Kingdom, Coming, whatever. This ends *now*.'

Matt and Rémy's rage rumbled in the air behind Em as she switched the kettle on. In her mind, she pressed their anger against the floor, bursting it like a balloon.

Rémy slouched in his chair and sighed.

Matt combed his fingers through his hair and pulled out a twig. He looked at it, and burst out laughing. He fired the stick at Rémy, who used it to fish his tea bag from his cup.

'Sorry,' Rémy said, smiling a little. 'I had no idea I could do that, raise the dead I mean.'

Em grinned to herself and poured water into her cup.

'Since we're all wide awake,' said Matt, 'we might as well get back to work.'

With Matt in the lead, they headed along the passageway into the church.

Rémy reached out and put his hand on Matt's shoulder. 'I've never lost control like that before.'

Matt put his hand on top of Rémy's. 'It happens.'

'What exactly were you doing up in the cemetery in the middle of the night anyway?' Em asked.

'I was revved up from the Piper. I thought I'd try to figure out more from my mom's diary,' Rémy began. 'That's when I heard them. The bagpipes.'

He retrieved his mother's journal from under the grate while Matt draped himself across an old armchair and wrapped himself in a tartan blanket. Em and Matt listened in silence as Rémy described how the music had lured him to the monument and pulled him down the narrow steps to the underground burial chamber of the Duke of Albion.

'He died in the sixteen hundreds.' Rémy looked at the others. 'Do you know who he was?'

'The Duke of Albion in the tomb was one of the founding members of Orion and one of our ancestors. But his family goes back to ancient times when his namesake was one of the first Animare, way back in the mists of forever,' said Em. 'You've heard of Oliver Cromwell, right?'

'Vaguely,' said Rémy.

'What?' scoffed Matt. 'No history in American schools?'

'You heard of Booker T. Washington?'

Em ignored them both. 'Cromwell was a dictator in the 1640s who chopped off the king's head and imposed his puritanical world-view on the country. The arts suffered, and Animare were caught up in the relentless round-ups by self-righteous Puritans and accused of sorcery or witchcraft. The Duke of Albion insisted the European Council of Guardians should get actively involved in the politics of the realm. He published a pamphlet known as the Albion Doctrine, and the European Council actually put him on trial for it.'

'Em,' said Matt, dropping his shades over his eyes as moonlight poured over him through the skylights. 'Ageing rapidly over here.'

'Anyway, the duke escaped Cromwell and the Council's clutches, and he and his followers formed Orion.' Em dragged a chair next to Rémy at the table. 'They operated in secret, kind of like the Underground Railroad did with slaves in America, only they were helping Animare to escape to safety. The Albion Doctrine has lots of haters to this day, and the Councils have never officially embraced it.'

Matt added, 'Although Orion, as a covert organization, has always embraced it.'

Rémy rubbed his hands together for warmth. 'And you didn't know this great white duke was buried up there?'

'Not sure I ever wondered or cared,' said Matt. 'But it makes sense.'

'Why seal him inside the monument?' asked Rémy. 'Why not give him his props in the official crypt beneath the church?'

'How do you know he was sealed inside?' asked Em.

'There was charcoal all over the door, and I think the crypt was sealed with some kind of ... of spell.'

'This isn't Hogwarts,' observed Matt.

'That's not what I meant and you know it,' said Rémy.

'Chill, both of you,' Em warned.

'I meant,' said Rémy, 'that someone may have bricked up that crypt, but it was an Animare that sealed it. I found charcoal all over the surface.'

'I need to see this crypt,' said Matt, standing up.

'Not happening,' said Em firmly. 'In the morning, maybe. But enough ghostbusting for tonight.'

28.

SOUND AND
VISION

M att picked up the old wooden chanter, examining the etchings on its silver collar. A circle of tiny thistles, like a crown of laurels, ran round the collar.

'Any idea why you in particular were drawn to that underground chamber?' he asked Rémy. 'Orion's been working from this church for centuries. Pretty sure no one's been called down there before now.'

'Pretty sure you've not had many Conjurors here either,' said Rémy.

'And pretty sure,' added Em, 'that the duke enchanted this pipe before he was sealed inside and somehow it reacted to Rémy's presence.'

'To what end?' asked Rémy.

'Maybe hoping some day someone like you would hear its call?'

'If that's the case,' said Rémy, 'then this etching must

mean something specific to a Conjuror. And so Matt's right. We do need to go back inside the monument.'

Matt carefully passed the instrument to Rémy, who ran his fingers over the glyphs. The chords cried in his head again, but this time a fleeting image, cherished and familiar, accompanied the sound.

'What?' said Em, alert to Rémy's expression.

'I saw something,' said Rémy.

Lifting his guitar case from a corner of the room, he dug around under his guitar until he found a photograph, which he pulled out and set on the table.

'I was eight or nine in this picture,' Rémy told the twins. 'We'd just moved to that apartment in Chicago. It was taken during one of my mom's good spells.'

'Your mum was beautiful,' said Em.

In the photograph, Rémy was presenting a birthday cake to a smiling Annie Dupree Rush. She was sitting at an old-fashioned roll-top desk covered in sheet music and her over-stuffed leather diary, the one now in Rémy's hand, was in her lap. She was smiling directly at the camera, a wide, open smile that made her eyes dance. Her hair was wrapped in a bright yellow scarf and the hoops in her ears made her look Bohemian and audacious at the same time. Every porthole in the desk was bulging with scraps of paper covered in scribbled notes. Multi-coloured Post-its were stuck all over the desk's surface.

'You have her eyes,' said Matt, who noticed everyone's eyes since the damage done to his own.

'Everyone says that,' said Rémy, his words catching in his throat. 'Look at the painting above the desk.'

Matt and Em peered at a painting of a teenage angel with velvety black wings playing the violin for Mary, Joseph and the baby Jesus.

'I never paid much attention to it,' Rémy said. 'But I remember Mom would never let anyone touch it. I just caught a glimpse of it when I touched that etching.'

'Let me see what I can find out about it,' said Em, opening Orion's database on a nearby computer. She tapped on a keypad next to the computer and a screen came down from the ceiling of the alcove. Then she tapped the computer and pulled up an image on the screen.

'That's the picture,' said Rémy, staring at the image of Mary holding Jesus while Joseph held the sheet music for the angel as if he was seeing it for the first time.

'It's called *Rest on the Flight into Egypt*,' said Em. 'According to Orion's description, it depicts the Holy Family beneath a copse of fruit trees after their escape from Herod.'

Matt and Rémy stared up at the image on the big screen. The angel was wrapped in flowing white gauze, his back bare and his black wings forefront in the composition, suggesting sensuality and mischief.

'According to these notes,' continued Em, 'the painting was a private commission for Cardinal Francesco Trastámara—'

Matt raised his hand to cut her off. 'The family who owned that village and palazzo in Spain where Rémy and I almost died last summer? The godfathers of the Camarilla?'

'The very one,' continued Em, her eyes sparking with interest. 'It says here that there were two versions of the painting. One is in a private collection in America, and the other has been missing for centuries. It's believed to have been one of the paintings stolen from the artist in the final days of his life.'

'Who's the artist?' asked Rémy, Em's adrenaline chiming in his head like tubular bells.

'Don't tell me,' said Matt, shaking his head.

'We have a winner,' said Em. 'The artist of *Rest on the Flight into Egypt* is Michelangelo Merisi de Caravaggio.'

29.

ARMED AND READY

'It can't be a coincidence that your mother had a copy of a Caravaggio hanging above her desk,' said Em, 'and he keeps popping up in our lives.'

'I don't think it's a copy,' said Rémy, his eyes still on the painting displayed on the screen.

Em stared. 'You think your mother had an *original* Caravaggio hanging in your flat in Chicago?'

'Hear me out,' said Rémy. 'We know my mom discovered the portrait of Cardinal Oscuro and the monster Don Grigori in the archives of the Dupree Plantation. Right?'

'Hardly likely to forget those two,' said Matt with feeling.

'She could have found, and taken, this picture at the same time,' Rémy said. 'The Duprees were art collectors. They had hundreds of paintings tucked away in their mansion.'

'Possible,' said Em, not yet convinced.

'What if my mom took it for insurance, to protect me?' Rémy went on. 'She knew Grigori and the Camarilla wanted to kill us—'

'Because,' Em cut in, 'the prophecy your mum discovered says a Conjuror is the only one who can stop the Watchers coming into the world to create their Second Kingdom.'

Rémy nodded. 'What if she knew this painting was crucial to that plan and she took it to trade for my life and her life some time in the future?'

'She also may just have liked it,' said Matt glibly.

Flipping quickly through the pages of his mom's journal, Rémy found what he was looking for and slid the page in front of the siblings. It was a torn catalogue page, folded and taped to the back of the journal.

'What are we looking at?' asked Matt, slipping his shades up into his hair, his eyes flashing from steel grey to a cold blue.

'It's the inventory of artefacts in the Dupree Plantation archives when they were sold.' Rémy tapped his finger at the middle of the list. 'Look. There.'

In the middle of the inventory was a long list of paintings, including *The Cardinal and His Disciple*, the double portrait now hidden somewhere in Rome. Beneath that was typed, *Rest on the Flight into Egypt* and a notation, *unaccounted for, assumed lost in passage*.

Em looked at the image on the screen again, at the angel's youthfulness and its black-feathered wings.

'So this painting travelled to America on a slave ship, along with the double portrait and whatever else the Camarilla was trying to hide,' she said.

'We know why the double portrait is important, but what's so important about this one?' Matt wondered.

'Is it because Caravaggio is the artist?' asked Em.

'I don't know,' said Rémy. 'But whatever the reason, I need to go home and get it.'

A soft yellow light began pulsing from the centre of a Turner painting on the wall: *Rome, from Mount Aventine*. The painting dominated the alcove where most of the paintings that Orion agents used to fade in and out of European galleries were hanging. Instantly an alarm clanged through the church. Someone was trying to fade in from Rome without Orion's permission.

Matt scrambled to his feet, grabbing a pen and a sketchpad from the table. Em ran to a keypad on the wall near the altar and silenced the alarm. Rémy took a position next to Matt in front of the Turner.

'Ready?' Matt asked.

Rémy's world had shifted on its axis the day his mom had died, and it appeared it was going to keep on tilting. He watched a winking light in the middle of the painting get brighter and brighter. With his harmonica cupped at his lips, he mumbled, 'This bad-ass ready to slay wit' da blues.'

In the painting, the wide bluish-white Tiber river flowed under the arches of the Ponte Emilio, down to the busy markets of the Trastevere on its bottom left. The river was bulging as if someone was pumping it with air, expanding and stretching, yellows, blues and greys flooding the ancient city's riverbanks. In a surge of sunlight and a rush of murky water, the arched bridge swung out of the painted space and dropped a drenched figure on to the alcove floor at Matt's feet.

'Speak of the devil,' said Matt, stomping his boot firmly on Caravaggio's sopping chest and pinning him to the ground. Rémy pinned the interloper's legs before he could spring to his feet. Em grabbed a roll of packing tape and quickly bound Caravaggio's hands together.

'Is this any way to greet a friend?' Caravaggio complained.

'You're not our friend,' growled Matt.

'Spy? Informant?' the artist suggested. 'Occasional lover?'

Matt growled louder, opening and closing his fists at his side. 'You've been wandering in painted space for too long,' he said. 'You've an over-inflated sense of your own worth. You're a liar and a thief and if not for your occasional intelligence-gathering for us, I would take great pleasure in—'

'You Scottish are too quick to anger, too fast to find faults,' said the artist reproachfully, struggling to his feet. 'Let's kiss and make up.'

Quick as lightning, the artist kicked out at Rémy. But Rémy was taller and younger, and pivoted away from the kick, charging his shoulders at Caravaggio, taking him down in front of the iron gate leading into the crypt. Matt swung the door open, and this time it was Rémy keeping Caravaggio on the floor with his knee on his chest.

The artist stopped smirking, raising his hands in the air. 'I surrender.'

'What are you doing here?' Matt said angrily.

'I thought it was time we joined forces and worked together to bring down the Camarilla once and for all.'

'We offered you a chance in Spain to work with us and you chose to take off instead,' said Rémy, pressing more of his weight on the artist's chest.

'I know, and that was rash of me, but I've had time to think,' Caravaggio said, trying unsuccessfully to shift to a better position beneath Rémy's knee.

'I'll ask again,' said Matt. 'What are you doing here?'

Caravaggio coughed, his face reddening. Rémy let up a little.

'Answer,' said Matt. 'Or he'll throw you into the crypt where you'll still answer our questions, but you'll be hurting more when you do.'

'Wait!' Em said, inserting herself into the mix. 'I get that he's an arrogant, deceitful dick, but he has been useful.'

With a grunt, Caravaggio rolled out from under Rémy and sat up. 'You're not going to hurt me,' he said with confidence. 'You're bluffing. You boys threaten;

she mollifies. You would all have lost your heads during the Inquisition,' he added. 'You are *attori terribli* ... such terrible actors.' He looked slyly at Rémy. 'And you may be a Conjuror, but you're weak.'

With both hands, Rémy rolled Caravaggio into the crypt. The artist howled as he crashed down the stone steps, swearing at them in Italian and English until he slammed into the ground.

'Probably shouldn't have done that,' panted Rémy to the siblings. 'But he was pissing me off.'

Down in the crypt, the artist moaned about cracking his forehead, but made no moves to scramble back up the steps.

'He'll be OK,' said Em. 'What about you?'

'I'm good,' said Rémy, hiding his emotions from Em with a jazz riff in his head until his muscles and his mind relaxed. He'd never been a fighter, but he wasn't about to admit that to Em, and certainly not to Matt. His family may have been poor and there may only have been the three of them, and Sotto Square, his landlord, but he'd always been protected. Their wealth had been their love. He was adrift now in a world he was struggling to understand, and no matter how hard Em tried to comfort him, Rémy knew he had to be the one to adjust himself to his new situation. He changed the subject.

'He's not going to stay there for long, you know,' Rémy said, looking down at the artist again. 'He'll draw his way out.'

'Maybe,' said Em, returning to the table. 'But I think he's staying. Whatever brought him here terrified him.'

'Then a crypt in the Highlands of Scotland might be the safest place for him right now,' said Matt, giving Caravaggio the finger as he slammed the iron gate closed.

30.

DROP SOME KNOWLEDGE

M att brought three fresh coffees from the kitchen. 'Thanks,' said Rémy, warming his hands on the steaming cup. 'Damn, it's cold and damp in here.'

'Welcome to Scotland,' said Matt. 'Land of freedom and frozen balls.'

'Listen to this, Rémy,' said Em, her fingers flying across the keyboard. 'After your mum took you to Chicago, the Dupree family archives were sold. The company that bought everything and shut the archives down was called Imperial Galleries. They have headquarters in London, Rome and Madrid. And,' she added with a grin and a dramatic flick of her fingers, 'one of their subsidiaries is Old Worm's Cabinet of Curiosities, where you tracked down the double portrait last summer.'

'How did you find that out so fast?' asked Rémy, sounding impressed.

'Learned from the best,' said Em. A surge of melancholy washed over her when she thought about the coding and computer tricks – some legal, some not so much – she'd picked up over the years from Zach. His tousled blond hair touching her ear as he leaned on her shoulder, his breath warm on her neck, his fingers pressing on top of hers as they'd chased code through cyberspace on one of the many computers he'd built from scratch.

Em sighed and typed a long string of code.

'Now we're getting somewhere,' she said, honing in on her prey. 'According to INTERPOL—'

'You've hacked into INTERPOL?' Rémy cut in, coughing up coffee.

'Not exactly,' said Em. 'Orion has a semi-legit portal to their files. Two Animare and their Guardians are on INTERPOL's Stolen Art Unit. Seems there is a file on missing works of art that have at some point in their provenance crossed with Imperial Galleries.'

Rémy put down his mug and stood behind Em. 'Can you see who owns the galleries?'

'Should be able to.'

Em scrolled through a page of code, tapped a few keys and a list of three names appeared on a page of Imperial Galleries' letterhead. She frowned.

'That's odd,' she said. 'Lucius Ferrante is listed as the company chairman, but that can't be right.'

'Who's Lucius Ferrante?' asked Rémy. 'Sounds like a celebrity chef.'

'In ancient Rome, Lucius Ferrante and his cult of followers were said to be more powerful than the emperor.'

Rémy looked blank.

'Roman scholars also considered him to be the father of alchemy because of his experiments with turning base metals to gold,' Em prompted.

'OK,' said Rémy, stretching the syllables.

'Weren't you paying attention to Snape in Potions class?'

'Don't encourage her,' said Matt, shaking his head.

'Plato mentions him a few times in his writing, so we're talking a *long* time ago,' Em continued. 'Think of Lucius Ferrante as the Rasputin of Emperor Hadrian's Roman court. The power behind the throne.'

'And the scary eyes,' added Matt, checking out his own reflection in his sunglasses.

'Like Rasputin, Lucius Ferrante wielded a strange control over the emperor's wife and sons,' Em went on. 'He was possibly one of the empress's lovers, or maybe one of her sons'. His apocryphal writings influenced *The Book of Enoch*, which was banned from the biblical canon because it was too out there.'

Rémy was about to interrupt, but Em held up a finger. 'But he's most renowned for compiling ways of moving between the natural and supernatural worlds.'

'Still having a hard time with that myself,' Rémy admitted.

'You must have known when you were a kid that your musical talent was beyond normal,' Matt said.

'It's hard to remember what I thought when I was a kid. I don't remember much from the years directly after my dad's death. And a lot of my adolescence was shrouded in secrets that I thought until recently had to do with my mom's mental illness. On good days, I thought I was a child prodigy.' Rémy paused. 'On bad ones, a freak of nature.'

Matt and Em glanced at each other. 'Freak of nature' was a label all too familiar to them.

'So what happened to this Ferrante dude?' asked Rémy.

'Hadrian tried to burn him at the stake,' said Em, with some relish. 'He tossed all his work on to the flames with him, but one of Ferrante's lovers stepped into the flames and rescued him, carrying him "unharmed from a fiery death" and "raised him up to the heavens", end quote. Of course, this miraculous event only made his cult stronger, and he became an even bigger threat to the emperor.' She paused. 'Now this is interesting…'

Her fingers clicked from one site to another, her concentration palpable, the air around her ticking with electricity.

'There's a reference in Orion's database that Lucius Ferrante's writings became part of the lost apocrypha the *Book of Songs*, which first prophesied the Second Kingdom. Parts of that book ended up in the *Book of Revelations* in the Bible.'

'Wait,' said Rémy. 'My mom has a note that the first reference to the Second Kingdom she could find was in a page from an ancient manuscript—' he flipped to a page in the old leather-bound journal – 'called the *Book of Songs*. It describes the prophecy. "Behold the Watchers, God's angels that fell from chaos. One day their kingdom will rule the earth … only a Conjuror shall cull them."'

'I knew we were on to something,' said Em in triumph.

Rémy smiled widely, and Em noticed for the first time that he had dimples.

'Do any of your sources tell us what happened to Ferrante, Em?' Matt asked.

'Eventually captured and locked away in a dungeon somewhere. No record of him after that.'

Matt took the journal from Rémy and looked at Annie Dupree Rush's notes.

'So Lucius Ferrante first writes about the Second Kingdom during Emperor Hadrian's reign,' he said. 'And ten years ago a company in his name buys the artefacts from the Dupree family archives.' He combed his fingers through his tangled hair. 'I appreciate the connections, Em, I do, but I'm not sure how they help us stop the Camarilla.'

'They help you,' said Caravaggio, lunging from the entrance to the crypt and thrusting his blade at Matt's throat, 'because Lucius Ferrante, or Luca as he is sometimes known, was … is … a nephilim. The offspring of a fallen angel and a human. The immortal Imperial Commander of the Camarilla, anointed to protect their cause and fulfil their prophecy.'

31.

MUSHY PEAS

Matt pitched forward, grabbed Caravaggio's forearm, twisted it and threw the artist to the ground. The knife clattered at Rémy's feet.

'Seriously,' said Rémy, picking up the knife and pointing it at the artist. 'Don't you ever play nice?'

Caravaggio sat up on his elbows, the gash at his forehead swelling. 'Force of habit.'

Matt dropped his shades to cover his kaleidoscopic eyes and hauled Caravaggio to his feet. He tore off the tape at his wrists and shoved him roughly on to a chair.

'I am hurting,' Caravaggio grumbled.

'Put this on your forehead,' said Em, impatiently handing Caravaggio the bag of now slightly less frozen peas that Matt had used earlier. She leaned in close and put her hands firmly on the artist's knees. The artist tilted his head to speak, but Em raised a finger to her lips, and nudged him back against the chair with the palm of her hand resting on his shoulder.

'I'm willing to ignore all the self-serving lies you've told us in the past,' she said, 'because when you faded here, you were terrified. I felt it. But if you want our help, we need to know everything you remember about your death, and everything you can remember about your life. No more flirting, no more attempts to seduce my brother...'

'Jesus, Em,' mumbled Matt.

'If the condom fits.'

'Can we save the sibling shaming for later?' Rémy enquired.

Rémy's emotions were screeching like out-of-tune guitars in Em's mind. He wasn't so much on edge, she thought, as hanging from a crumbling cliff one-handed. She squeezed Caravaggio's shoulders, increasing her psychic pressure, sending a calm soft blue under his skin.

'We need to know what scared you and why,' she said gently.

Caravaggio closed his eyes. Em felt his muscles relax beneath her hands.

'When I first came to Rome,' he began, 'poverty blinded me. My hunger fed my work, my form was lacking, my figures clumsy, hands out of proportion, eyes dead. But then I met my saviour. At least, that's what I thought at the time.'

'Em, we don't have time for his life story,' hissed Matt.

Em silenced her brother with a look. But Caravaggio had tensed and his eyes had flown open. She couldn't tell if he'd seen something and didn't want to share, or if his memory had shut down again. He wriggled away from her hands and stood up, his hands rubbing at his temples.

'I do not need your inspiriting, my love,' he said to Em. 'I will tell you what I remember. It is the truth. I swear, but my head is still hurting. Would you have a little liquor to ease the pain?'

Em reached for the bottle of whisky that lived on Vaughn's desk and pressed it into the artist's hands. Caravaggio inhaled the rich smells of the liquid, nodded his approval and drank.

'The memories of the day I supposedly died have been locked away from me for centuries,' he said, setting down the bottle reluctantly. 'I understand, after spending time in this century, that my inability to access my memories is a consequence of something called "post-traumatic stress". Now I find myself remembering.'

Outside the sun was rising, ribbons of soft light dipping in through the skylights.

'I had taken something from Luca Ferrante,' he said, 'and I was dying from a stab wound. I was rescued by a friend and taken north. But Luca was catching up. He wanted what I had taken from him, and he would stop at nothing to get it back. My rescuer threw me from the carriage we were travelling in. I rolled down the hillside into water. And I remember … somehow, as the water was closing over my head, I was taken up by some kind of force. Everything went dark.'

Em, Matt and Rémy leaned closer as Caravaggio's hands trembled on the bottle.

'On waking, I somehow found myself inside a painting by Pieter Bruegel the Elder. There were bodies climbing all over me, howling and screaming, and the smell of sulphur and burning flesh. I knew I was no longer bleeding from the wound at my side, or dying for that matter, but I was suffocating. I wasn't meant to be in that painted space. Its very essence, its gravity was fighting me. I knew if I didn't fade fast, I'd soon be dead.'

Rémy poured more whisky. Caravaggio gulped it, wiping his mouth with the open cuff of his sleeve. Matt took out his sketchpad and began making notes and doodles.

'I used everything I had left and I faded back into the real world,' Caravaggio said. 'I felt as if I had been away for minutes, but discovered that it had been centuries. Five to be exact.

'I was in a gallery where the walls were crowded with art. Paintings hanging from floor to ceiling. I could hear angry voices. I didn't think I had much time. On the other side of the room, I saw another Bruegel and I could see it had an open exit.'

Rémy opened his mouth.

'A painting with an exit to another work has a distinctive glow and it must have a painting in it,' Em explained. 'Orion has mapped out most of the ones we use in our database, and we know where we're heading before we leave.'

'But you can fade into any painting you want, right?'

'We can, but if it doesn't have an exit then you're caught in the world of that art.'

Caravaggio continued. 'I eventually faded into one of my own works, *The Martyrdom of St Matthew,* where unfortunately I faded too hard and hit my head, losing most of my memories of who... and what I'd done. Now those memories have returned.' He gazed at Rémy with intense curiosity. 'The Camarilla are offering a reward for you,' he said.

'What's the reward?' said Matt.

'A shitload of cash, as you in this vulgar world would say.' The artist paused, glancing again at Rémy. 'Or eternal life in the Second Kingdom.'

32.

THE TRIUMPH
OF DEATH

'Are you sure you were bound inside a Bruegel?' asked Em.

'Do not doubt my knowledge of the masters, my love,' said Caravaggio. 'I've been inside many of them.' His eyes gleamed. 'In fact...'

'Don't go there,' Matt ordered. 'Em, the painting has to be *The Triumph of Death*.'

Em typed the name into the image database and the painting appeared on the screen. She hit enlarge and print. In seconds, a full-colour quality copy of the painting shot out of a printer. Matt tore down posters from a job involving Banksy that two other agents were working on and pinned the Bruegel on the wall.

Caravaggio's astonishment sent threads of gold and shades of light and dark through Em's imagination. She grabbed Matt's charcoal and quickly sketched the image that flooded her mind.

'My God, it is even more horrific than I remember,' the artist said, staring at the painting on the screen.

Em grabbed Caravaggio's arm. 'Who is this woman?' she asked, shoving the sketch she'd drawn from his imagination under his nose.

Caravaggio stared at the sketch, all colour draining from his face. His fear – no, his *terror* – hit Em like ice water.

'Who is she?' she repeated.

'Her name,' Caravaggio whispered, 'is Sebina. Luca's soulmate. Helen to his Paris, Chloe to his Daphnis, Eve to his Adam. She is a nephilim like Luca, but perhaps even more powerful.'

SECOND MOVEMENT

'And behold those who serve
shall take human form.'

Book of Songs

33.

DANGEROUS CROSSING

ROME, 1610

Below the rocky embankment where Caravaggio stood, a girl of no more than eighteen dragged a raft from the undergrowth and slid it into the shallows of the river. She waded in, holding the raft steady with her hands. Dawn was hours away.

'*Signore*, it is safe,' she called up to the artist.

A light breeze rustled the trees, a merchant's wagon stacked with barrels of wine and its team of horses rolled past on the packed dirt road, peals of laughter and drinking songs carried from revellers falling out of the closing taverns nearby. A handful of drunken sailors chased each other out on to the Pons Fabricius directly above the girl and her raft, where they howled at the moon and pissed into the river. The noises of the eternal city were familiar to Caravaggio, comforting even, but on this night Rome sounded apprehensive, the voices hollow and strained, the horses snorting too loudly, the laughter forced.

Cloaked like a monk with a leather satchel strapped across his chest, Caravaggio slid down the hill towards the girl, grasping at branches with his free hand, trying to keep his balance. His other hand gripped a bolt of fabric wrapped in sackcloth.

At the shore, the girl yanked a knife from the waistband of her woollen leggings, holding the blade out in front of her. Lippita's skill with a knife was legendary. That, together with her mother's connections to the Medici and the Borgias, had kept Lippita in business on the river longer than most. Rome operated on favours and false promises, conspiracies and confidences, and the Tiber, navigated by young people like Lippita, was the conduit that carried them between princes and popes.

'Were you followed?' she asked.

'No,' said Caravaggio, pausing for a breath. 'I was extra cautious. You can put that away.'

Lippita's lithe body was mostly muscle, except for the thick black hair that she kept short and always hidden beneath her skullcap. Like Caravaggio, she had blackened her face with soot. She slid her knife away reluctantly.

'Your mother,' Caravaggio asked, still feeling his way down the bank. 'She is well?'

Lippita spat into the river. 'As well as you might expect.'

Lippita's mother had posed for Caravaggio more

than once: his infamous Virgin Mary. But like many of the city's unwanted children, Lippita had raised herself, her mother an infrequent presence in her life.

Two fat water rats with mangy rumps scuttled from the undergrowth in front of Caravaggio and darted across the rocks, making him snort in disgust. The banks of the Tiber were swarming with them. Rats were about the only things living on the river that were not starving. That was why these secret journeys in the middle of the night were necessary evils. Payment for one journey out of the city would feed Lippita for a week.

Lippita kicked one of the rats, sending it on a high arc into the water. It landed with a loud splash. Caravaggio froze, gripping a tree with his free hand. He worried it may have called attention to their passage.

Lippita shrugged, as if reading his mind. 'No one will notice the splash of a rat. But, *signore*, we must hurry if you are to make your connection.'

Caravaggio slid down the final few yards of the embankment on his bottom.

'It is an honour, *signore*,' Lippita said, helping Caravaggio to his feet. 'Mamma adores you.'

'And I she,' said Caravaggio, kissing Lippita's cheeks. They were warm, despite her being dressed in only a thin belted tunic and woollen leggings. Clouds crept across the moon, and darkness enveloped them. Lippita let her raft bob out into the current.

'We need more light,' Caravaggio said, fumbling his way over the rocks to the river's edge, holding the bolt of fabric high above his head. 'I can take care of that.'

'No,' Lippita said. 'They may see the glow of your magic. I will manage.'

'But how?'

'I was born on this river,' said Lippita assuredly. 'I know its switches and turns blindfolded. You first, *signore*.'

The raft rocked as Caravaggio settled cross-legged in the middle. Lippita had over-estimated his weight, and tossed two sandbags she'd filled earlier on to the front for better balance. She climbed aboard with barely a ripple, and used her long oar to push them out into the current.

'Will the canvas be safe in that roll?' she asked, nodding at the bolt.

'I will guard it with my life,' Caravaggio replied.

Lippita punted them past a line of tugs pulling massive blocks of marble strapped to rafts ten times the size of hers. They were heading towards Vatican City, the red ash from the captain's pipe illuminating his skeletal face in a ghostly light that reminded Caravaggio of how difficult a dance the play of light and dark could be in both real and painted space.

He sighed, his actions weighing as heavily on him as the bolt of fabric.

'I can take your burden from you if you'd like,' offered Lippita.

'Oh, my sweet child, don't waste your worry on me,'

he said, hugging the parcel tighter to his chest. 'When I get this canvas out of the reach of the Camarilla, I'll sleep better.'

'Where will you hide, *signore*, that they cannot reach?' Lippita's oar entered the water silently and skilfully as she kept the raft steady in the wake of the tugs. 'The Camarilla has spies everywhere.'

Caravaggio found himself relaxing for the first time in days under the soft rocking of the raft. 'I've arranged for my passage north,' he told her. 'It seems there are others fighting to keep hidden what the Camarilla seek.'

The girl wiped her brow with her sleeve and rowed on. She nodded at the bolt of cloth. 'Is that one of them?'

Surprised at the question, Caravaggio glanced up at her. A strange sensation tingled through him. Slowly, he slid the bolt of cloth between his knees, balancing it on the top of his feet, keeping it from touching the seeping wet planks at the bottom of the raft. He tightened his right hand on the hilt of his sword.

'This,' he said softly, 'this is my insurance contract.'

They were gliding past Trastevere now, its roadside torches burning less brightly as the night deepened, their dying flames barely illuminating the poet Dante's palace, its facade crumbling under the occupation of an indifferent descendant.

'Lippita, were you ever baptized?' he asked, leaning forward, hoping his question might distract her watchful eye from the bolt of cloth.

'A strange question, *signore*,' said Lippita warily, digging her oar into the murky depths, propelling them away from the thickening barge traffic. 'I was baptized in this very river.'

'Ah, of course,' said Caravaggio. He paused, anxiously raising his hand. 'Halt! Do you hear that?'

She opened her mouth to reply, but Caravaggio held a finger to his lips. They floated on the current as voices, high and clear, drifted to them from above the bend of the river.

'It's the castrati from St Peter's,' whispered Lippita, stabbing her oar into the water. 'They are readying for lauds.'

'Not that,' said Caravaggio, standing cautiously, the raft rocking beneath him. 'That.'

He pointed at the canopy of trees overhead, bending and rustling. He held his finger up. There was no wind on the river.

'It is nothing.' Lippita turned the raft into the shore-line, her shoulders tautening beneath her tunic. 'Your rendezvous is here at this bend.'

But for Caravaggio she had been too quick to answer, too quick to dismiss his concerns. His every muscle tensed and he held the bolt like a sceptre to steady his balance. Water slapped over his feet, splashing the fabric.

On the shore, the trees bowed in supplication, letting the moonlight glisten on the shallow water as if stars were falling.

34.

RISE UP!

The closer the raft got to the muck of the shoreline, the louder the rustling in the trees became, their limbs whipping violently. Yet the water was calm. It was impossible to ignore the racket any longer.

'Perhaps the Cardinal has lost his circus bear,' Lippita suggested.

'Only if the bear has climbed into the trees,' replied Caravaggio.

This section of the river served the largest population of Rome, their shit flowing in torrents into the water. A rat scuttled across the rocks with a smaller rat locked in its jaw. Another, then another followed, abandoning the embankment like a sinking ship.

'Something is out there,' said Caravaggio. 'This place is compromised. Take us from here.'

Hundreds of rats, layers upon layers of them, were sliding into the mud now, snarling and snapping at each other's necks and tails to get deeper into the water.

'*Signore*, your carriage will be waiting,' Lippita insisted. 'I am not travelling any further with you.'

Another chilling gust of wind flattened the trees completely, its force knocking Caravaggio into Lippita. She struggled to keep her raft from being submerged under a wave of sludge, shoved him aside and dropped prostrate on to the raft. Rats teemed across her back and legs. Not one bit or scratched her.

'Dear God,' breathed Caravaggio. 'Who are you? What have you done?'

Securing the bolt of fabric under his feet, he drew his sword and held its tip to Lippita's skin. A drop of blood dribbled down the long curve of her neck on to the raft, where it sizzled lightly. Rats tore at his hem, their teeth ripping into the flesh at his calf.

'Get up,' Caravaggio snarled. 'You—'

Lippita leaped, driving her knife to the hilt into Caravaggio's side, twisting twice before removing it. The artist fell backwards into the shallow water. She grabbed the bolt of cloth before it rolled from the raft.

Caravaggio floundered. With heavy limbs and the muck holding him in its stink, he was just able to keep his head above the water. More rats swam past him, over him, under him, until he found himself carried out into the channel on their backs.

Above the trees, a beast revealed itself, hovering like a prehistoric dragonfly above the crouching canopy. The music he'd heard earlier, the choir of boys, was now only one voice, seductive and sensual, and Caravaggio felt himself give in to its will.

He swallowed and the muck burned his throat as the creature descended on to Lippita's raft, the sound of its great double wings like a thousand swarming bees.

Caravaggio's mind was in rapture. Visions of Tomas, his favourite model, and others like him reached into the artist's core, caressing him, loving him. With his body sinking deeper into the dirt he lifted his hand mindlessly to Tomas's cheek.

A rat snapped at his fingers. Searing pain shot up his arm, and Tomas vanished, leaving Caravaggio choking in the flotsam. He had to shut his mind and get away from this creature and its illusions. With a painful gasp, he dragged himself into a channel of waste pouring from the streets above, positioning his body behind a knot of twisted tree roots.

The winged creature sat up on its haunches and reached out to Lippita. Caravaggio's terror strangled the air from his lungs, urine warmed his breeches, the wound on his side pulsed his life into the Tiber.

Lippita was floating above the raft now, in the arms of a winged man more magnificent than Michelangelo's David, whose every muscle and limb seethed with a desire that made Caravaggio's body ache. The creature's forewings folded in thick dark layers against his wide back, his hind wings remaining erect.

'My love,' the creature crooned. He crushed Lippita

against his chest, and a soft moan escaped her lips as her ribs snapped and her spine pierced her tunic.

The creature laid her with great care on the raft. He slipped off her skullcap, combed his tapered fingers through her short dark hair, then crouched over her like a bird with its prey as rats surged on to her broken body.

The creature's forewings opened. A ball of pale yellow light ballooned from the centre of Lippita's shredded carcass and the creature's hands worked the light like a sculptor manipulating clay. The creature's wings enveloped the raft and for a moment there was only darkness. When it opened its wings again, a vision rose from Lippita's body like Botticelli's Venus.

Caravaggio gasped in awe.

'Sebina, my love,' whispered the winged creature. 'The artist? Where is he?'

'He matters not. He is already food for the rats with my knife in his side.'

'Are you certain?'

Sebina stretched out her arms, her jet-black hair falling on her brown skin. 'Do you doubt me?'

He came to her. Their embrace sent drops of light out across the Tiber like a million incandescent beads on a wedding gown. It was as intimate as anything Caravaggio had ever witnessed, the passionate entwining of their limbs as pure as it was dangerous.

Caravaggio scrawled a flagon of wine on the rocks for what he felt sure would be his last drink on this earth.

He drank the animation with gusto, clutching his satchel against the crushing pain in his heart and head.

With Sebina in his arms and the artist's bundle of cloth in hers, the winged creature rose to the heavens and for a brief moment the two of them were silhouetted against the horned moon. Deep in the weeds, Caravaggio was dimly aware of someone dragging him from the muck.

'Come, my friend,' said a voice. 'Ah've a wagon waiting.'

35.

CALCULUS NOT THE WORST

'Jesus,' said Matt, the mug of coffee sloshing in his grip. 'How could you not remember that?'

'How could you *not* forget it?' said Em, her pale skin even whiter. 'I think I'm going to be sick.'

She darted down the hallway to the kitchen. The others waited in silence until she returned, bringing bottles of water with her.

'So this creature,' said Matt. 'It's here? In the twenty-first century?'

'Yes. Lucius – Luca – Ferrante is here,' said Caravaggio.

'Ferrante?' repeated Rémy. 'The Roman guy, the immortal Commander of the Camarilla? He has wings?'

'He is a nephilim,' said Caravaggio. 'Half angel, half human. When he is in his angel form he has wings and is massive in stature. He's here to take back what I stole from him and his Camarilla.'

'But he got the bolt of fabric,' said Matt, puzzled.

'What I kept from him was not in the fabric. That was a diversion suggested by the man who saved me that day, the man I was supposed to be meeting on the embankment. All Luca got was a cheap bolt of wool.'

'What happened to Sebina?' asked Matt. 'The one who killed Lippita and used her body?'

Caravaggio stood and stretched. 'I only saw Luca emerge from my canvas this morning in Rome. Not Sebina. I do not know her fate. But this morning in Rome when Luca appeared to me, I remembered who he was ... and what I'd done for him.'

'What exactly *had* you done for him?'

'I sold my powers to the Camarilla as a young man.'

'I knew you couldn't be trusted,' hissed Matt, sweeping his hand over the table, sending papers and Post-its flying.

'I did what I needed to do to survive,' the artist replied, stabbing the air in front of Matt's face with his finger. 'I was never as strong as you and your sister, and I knew nothing of Guardians or places of sanctuary until I was rescued from the Tiber river that night. But you need to know this, and to believe it. In this century, in your lifetimes, I've never betrayed my kind.'

'Let me get this clear,' said Rémy. 'If this half-man, half-angel creature, Luca, is working for the Watchers and their Second Kingdom, then why is he jonesing for you and not me? I'm the only one who can stop them, right?'

'It's not that simple,' said the artist. 'The prophecy suggests the Conjuror can choose.'

'Choose what?'

'To destroy the Second Kingdom,' Caravaggio replied, 'or to create it. I think Luca believes he can convince you to help him.'

There was a long silence.

'Shit,' said Rémy. 'I really miss the days when I thought calculus would kill me.'

'The Camarilla need three items to build their Second Kingdom.' Caravaggio ticked off the three on his fingers. 'One: a Conjuror. Two: a golden lyre. And three: the sacred chord, sometimes known as the Devil's Interval, for the Conjuror to play upon the lyre. We are closer than they are to finding these things. We have you already, Rémy. And I remembered when I saw Luca this morning that I had hidden the sacred chord in one of my paintings.'

'And the lyre?' asked Em.

Caravaggio shook his head. 'I was looking for that when we first met. I have had no luck yet.'

'A'right, now we're getting somewhere,' exclaimed Rémy. He hit the space bar on the computer. 'Is this the painting where you hid the sacred chord?'

Caravaggio looked up at the screen, at the Holy Family and the black-winged angel. At the music on the music stand. 'Ah, such exquisiteness, such beauty. My Tomas. He was always my best angel. His back, his arms…' He kissed his fingertips. 'Such perfection.'

Rémy waved his two fingers in front of the artist's eyes. 'Focus!'

'Yes,' said the artist. 'This is the one.'

'We need to go to Chicago and get that painting,' said Rémy. 'I'm not waiting around for the Camarilla or this Ferrante dude to come find me first.'

Em stood up and embraced him. 'It's going to be hard for you,' she said softly.

'I can handle fear,' he told the top of her pink-and-black head. 'It's just that when I fled, I didn't even have time to bury my family...'

'I'm sure your friend, Sotto, took care of them,' said Em.

'I know he did. But I don't want Sotto and his family fighting my battles any more. We need to get that painting – and destroy it.'

36.

REWIND

Caravaggio stood in front of his painting on the screen, the sun's early light diffusing through the room like flickering candles. There was a lot of the twenty-first century that he liked: devices that played music, paint in squeezable tubes, paper in colours that didn't need to be treated for days, soft wipes in flushing water closets, fresh fruit on demand. But what shocked him every day when he faded through modern Paris, Florence, Rome, Madrid and Milan, the cities of his life, was how the people with whom he'd populated his art so long ago – the poor, the forgotten, the exploited – were no less disposable or poor than they had been in his time. He found it difficult to fathom, and disappointing to know, that the poor had successfully stormed only a handful of Bastilles since his time.

'I first saw Luca Ferrante at the wedding for Count Marche's youngest daughter,' he began. 'He cornered me in the library and made me an offer I couldn't refuse.'

'Rewind,' said Matt with a snort. 'You could have refused, but you didn't.'

'I couldn't refuse,' Caravaggio repeated, 'because hunger was gnawing at my gut and vanity was squeezing my soul. I needed patronage and porridge. When I looked into his eyes, I thought at first he was a Guardian sent to reprimand me for my public displays of animation. At that time they were mostly related to my physical needs. Which are many, I might add.'

Em sighed.

'I bound the sacred chord in this painting as Luca Ferrante asked. He and the Camarilla used me for smaller imaginings, but hiding this chord bought me my largest commission. However, when a dear friend enlightened me on the Second Kingdom and the prophecy in the *Book of Songs* – well. You might say I got cold feet.'

'And,' said Em, disgust shading her tone, 'your humanity rose to the surface?'

'Let's just say my heart was convinced,' Caravaggio said, annoyed at her tone. 'You and your brother would have done the same in my circumstances. Hunger is a powerful motivator.' He eyed Matt. 'As is sex.'

Rémy was rifling around in his guitar case. 'I'll call Sotto and let him know we're coming to Chicago,' he said. 'Do you guys have passports?'

Caravaggio laughed. 'You three are precious. A nephilim is chasing me across time for a scrap of music I hid in a painting. A painting that likely got your mother killed, Rémy. This nephilim also has the entire Camarilla looking for you both. And you think travel papers will get you back to the New World?'

'Would you stop calling it the New World?' said Rémy. 'It was populated before any of your people got there.'

'So you say, my friend,' said the artist, softening his tone but hardening his expression. 'Just remember this. The sheet music is useless to the Camarilla if they don't have their hands on a Conjuror or the sacred instrument. Going to Chicago might put you into their hands. That is one third of the battle won. Are you sure it's the best move?'

'It doesn't matter whether it is or it isn't,' said Rémy. 'It's the move I'm making. I'm tired of running away. My mom spent her life looking over her shoulder. I don't want to live that way any more.' He smiled at Matt and Em. 'Besides, I have the best Animare in the world on my side.'

Matt went into the kitchen, opened the freezer and lifted out a portable safe from under a frozen lasagne. 'A key, please, Em,' he said.

Em went to the whiteboard, and in a splash of copper a key appeared in the lock of the safe. Matt popped it open and counted out three hundred dollars. He closed the safe as Em erased the drawing.

'If you have decided to go,' said Caravaggio with a shrug, 'there is nothing more that I can do but drink and hope that you succeed.' He lifted Vaughn's whisky from the coffee table and stretched himself out under Matt's tartan blanket. 'I shall be comforted by your scent, young Matt, until you return with my art.'

Matt threw a stapler at him.

'OK,' Em said. 'No phones. We don't need anyone tracking us.'

The three of them tossed their phones on the coffee table. Em logged on to the Orion database and opened a secure file, labelled ART HISTORY. She typed fast, scrolling down only once. 'I've got the paintings we need to use to fade,' she said. 'Use the landline, Rémy, and tell Sotto to meet us outside the Art Institute in Chicago.'

Matt looked worried. 'That's a long way, Em. Are you sure?'

'No, but I have faith in us.'

'If time remains constant when an Animare fades,' Caravaggio mumbled, well on his way to a drunken stupor, 'it stands to reason that distance may hold too. Or at least shrink.'

Matt shrugged. 'I guess we're going to Chicago, then.'

Rémy made the call.

37.

TRAINS, PLANES
AND PAINTINGS

Matt darted round the traffic on Princes Street in Edinburgh. His hip clipped the edge of a Fiat. The driver blared his horn. Matt didn't stop until he reached the pavement on the other side. Rémy and Em crossed at the traffic lights.

'I thought we were in a hurry,' Matt said when Rémy and Em finally caught up.

'We are in enough danger as it is,' snapped Em. 'I do not plan to get taken out by a Hibs fan.'

A few minutes later they were inside the Scottish National Gallery, taking the lift to the top floor. When the doors closed, Em pulled out the stop button used by curators to hold the lift.

'Maybe we should split up?' Rémy suggested. 'Two of us go to Chicago while one stays in Scotland? If I'm wrong about the painting, someone needs to warn Orion.'

'We need to do this together,' said Matt. 'We've never been to Chicago, and you may need help when you get there.'

'I don't need your help,' Rémy began, bristling.

'Boys,' said Em, stepping between them. 'This is getting old. And I'm tired of being the peacemaker. So here's the deal. We will all go to Chicago. Matt will need the help fading. It's a long way, and—'

Someone thumped on the lift doors.

'Are you OK in there?' a female voice asked. 'Is the lift stuck?'

The twins recognized the voice as belonging to one of the volunteer tour guides in the museum who was not aware of Orion. Em hit the button and the lift began its ascent to the upper floor. Cutting round a school group filing into the French Impressionist gallery, the three sprinted to Edouard Vuillard's *La Chambre Rose*.

'We'll need to be fast, Matt,' warned Em.

'You look worried,' said Rémy.

'Wee bit,' said Em. 'Vuillard left parts of this painting unfinished. It was a technique he used for texture and depth. He also liked—'

'Short-story version,' interrupted Matt. 'If we fade into an unfinished spot, we can get stuck. Permanently.'

'The train to London is sounding more appealing by the second,' Rémy said.

'The painting on Vuillard's bedroom wall will take us to the National Gallery in London,' Em told him.

'We can fade from the Seurat there to the Art Institute in Chicago.'

'Do it,' said Rémy, taking Em's hand.

Matt flipped open his sketchpad and began to draw. Em placed her hand on his shoulder. In an instant her imagination pushed its power towards his, creating a cloak of pale white light around the three of them. Matt's fingers skated across the page, sparks of brilliant colour shooting through his fingers. Em's limbs felt like they were melting. Rémy burst into light first.

38.

A SMALL PRICE
TO PAY

The guards rushed into the gallery seconds after the three had faded.

'Nora was sure there was something strange about those teenagers,' said the first guard, looking around.

'So where the hell did they go?' asked the second guard in a puzzled voice.

The first guard stepped closer to Vuillard's *La Chambre Rose*. He ran his foot over marks on the floor. Kneeling, he stuck his finger into the stain. With a yelp, he yanked his finger away.

'What is it?' said his partner.

'It's bloody hot.' The guard lifted his finger to his nose and sniffed. 'Smells like turpentine.'

'We should raise the alarm.'

The first guard was still on his knees, looking up at the painting when the blow came. His partner was scrambling for his radio when he was hit as well. He rolled beneath the electronic eye and set off the alarm. The gallery doors began to slide shut.

Nora Patterson, part-time tour guide for the Scottish National Gallery, hitched up her skirt and slid underneath a gate as it dropped. Then she straightened her blouse and walked smartly to the stairs, where she helped the teachers get the schoolchildren out of the door and into the park. A busload of pensioners needed assistance getting outside, so that it was at least a half-hour before she could head to the coffee shop beneath the gallery.

She spotted him at a table in the corner behind a shelf of gallery souvenirs, nursing a cup of hot chocolate. He smiled when she pulled out the seat in front of him, then drew a half-circle and three slashes across the creamy foam on top. Nora recognized the shape with a thrill of adrenaline. It matched the tattoo on the taut muscle above his hipbone. Alerting him to any strange coming and goings at the gallery was a small price to pay for the pleasure he gave her in return.

Luca reached over and set his hands on top of hers. Nora felt such a surge of desire, she squirmed a little on the chair.

'I can't stop shaking,' she said, setting her trembling hands flat on the glass tabletop. 'I did what you asked. Oh God, what if I've killed those two guards?'

He carefully wiped the cream from his finger with the edge of a napkin. She noticed the napkin was covered in strange doodles and Roman numerals, a little Latin tucked among the scribbles.

'Your reward will be doubled, my love,' he said. 'You've done well. Now tell me again exactly where they said they were going?'

Nora hadn't felt this giddy in years. Every sense was heightened. She could hear the most beautiful melody in her head: a flute, sensual and seductive, drowning out the sirens from outside. She inhaled his scent in gulps. He smelled of spice and musk and something indescribable.

She felt his hand on her hips, her skirt sliding up her thighs as he lifted her on to the table, his body pressing against her, his soft lips kissing her. She gasped. People might see, but she didn't care.

'On the floor!'

The guide found herself thrown to the ground. A police officer in full riot gear put her boot on her back.

'What's happening?' Nora gasped. Her heart thumped in her chest as she remembered the sound as the two guards fell after she hit them. Her vision was blurring. Vomit rose in her throat.

Oh God, what had she done?

'Stay still!'

'I'm going to be sick,' she moaned.

The officer pulled her on to her knees. 'Go ahead.'

She turned her head, her body wrenching until she had nothing left. The officer dragged her to her feet. Two other officers, also in riot gear, had circled the table.

'She assaulted two of the museum's guards,' said a female officer. 'Gallery got an anonymous tip she also planted explosives.'

'That's absurd,' moaned Nora, tears choking her as she looked around. 'It's his fault. I would never...'

Luca was gone.

Nora fought against the restraints tight on her wrists. 'Did you get him?' she said piteously. 'He paid me to do it.'

'Who?'

'His name is...' Suddenly she couldn't remember. 'He was here! I swear.'

A crowd gathered outside the windows. One of the security guards was pointing at Nora from inside an ambulance, a medic holding ice at his head, and all she could think was: at least I didn't kill them.

She struggled as the police officers round her hooked their arms under her shoulders and grabbed her feet. They carried Nora screaming through the glass doors, with the café staff gawking at her from behind the pastry counter.

'You saw him,' she sobbed at the waiters. 'He was at the table with me. Tell them.'

The two waiters shrugged.

'You have to tell them. He was drinking hot chocolate.'

Nora was shoved into the back of a police van and strapped into a seat harness, her hands cuffed on her lap.

'Wait! This is a terrible mistake,' she cried. 'I never

meant to hurt them. It was his idea… he paid me to watch the paintings.'

The steel doors slammed on her words. She flopped as far forward as the seat harness allowed and tears burst from her in gulping waves.

She heard the melody first. The flutes. The caressing thrum of a cello. *Oh Jesus, Jesus*, she thought helplessly to herself, *what's happening to me?* Her heart thumped. Her pulse raced. Then her blood pressure spiked and she burst into flames.

THIRD MOVEMENT

'And Behold the Watchers shall rise
from whence they are bound.'

Book of Songs

39.

IN THE JUNGLE

Sotto Square was heading north on Michigan Avenue in front of the Art Institute of Chicago in his grandmother's pristine 1979 Cadillac Fleetwood. He was cruising slowly. It was two in the morning in Chicago's Gold Coast, and traffic was thin, but Sotto wasn't in a rush. The last train had trundled beneath Michigan Avenue ten minutes ago, and most of the bars and clubs in the central loop were closed or closing. Clusters of men and women waited at the bus stops along Michigan Avenue, and in the distance, the DuSable Bridge over the Chicago River was up, yellow lights flashing.

A barefoot, homeless woman was pushing a shopping cart piled with black garbage bags out of the Art Institute's south garden and on to the sidewalk. She yelled up at the prowling lion, one of two huge bronze lions in different poses that flank the wide entrance.

A lone pedestrian walked out of Millennium Park and headed west, his collar popped, his hands deep in his camel-coat pockets, a stocking cap on his head. Sotto was watching the pedestrian with interest when, without warning, two joggers cut across the thin line of traffic in front of his Caddy. He hit his brakes and then his horn. The pedestrian kept walking without a backwards glance.

'Way to be stealthy, man,' Sotto muttered as he cruised past the building, slapping his hand on the wheel and cursing himself.

He looked at his watch. They should be here soon. Rémy had called from a pay phone in London to give him a heads up that they were close. He decided to circle the block again and keep his eye on the man in the camel coat. Heading west on Adams, he turned right on Wabash, driving under the empty elevated tracks. This time when he came round on to Michigan from the other direction, he noticed the Art Institute block was surrounded by fog, yet somehow the other buildings and the street in front were clear. The homeless woman was dumpster-diving at the side of the building, her cart parked on the grass while the man in the camel coat walked through the fog. Sotto cut in front of a bus and pulled the Caddy into its lane to get a closer look at the man's face. But he had to keep moving, and the bus was tight on his fender. In his rear-view mirror, he could see the driver giving him the finger. When he refocused on the pedestrian, he couldn't see him.

He swerved the Caddy out of the bus lane and let the bus pass, then did a tight U-turn and doubled back.

Streamers of bluish-green fog fluttered around the building's façade, engulfing the bronze lions. Sotto blinked and shook his head. Had one of the lions stretched its neck and looked towards him?

Nah. Getting paranoid.

Sotto had taken his eyes off the road for only a second, but when he turned back, the homeless woman's cart was trundling into the street with the woman chasing behind it, mumbling and waving her hands in the air. Sotto slammed on his brakes and swerved to avoid her and her cart. In the instant he pulled the wheel he realized the terrible mistake he'd made. The homeless woman was waving a gun.

Bang. Bang.

A long *wheeesh,* like bullets hitting his car.

The Caddy jumped the kerb and hit a Free Press newspaper box, folding the flimsy metal beneath its front fender. Across the street beneath the curve of the L, Sotto glimpsed a Chicago police car lighting up and turning on to Michigan Avenue. He scrambled from the front seat. Reaching under the fender, he tried to dislodge the metal box.

'Goddammit,' he said aloud. Even if he could get it to budge, his two front tyres were flat.

The CPD car cut across the traffic and into his lane.

'Sir, put your hands where we can see them. And step away from your vehicle.'

Sotto did what he was asked. Dangerous not to.

He stared in disbelief at the Art Institute. The homeless woman was disappearing into the haze hanging over the entire front of the building like a shimmering net. The lions were twitching, their paws lifting off their pedestals as if they were tearing themselves free.

40.

MY KIND
OF TOWN

Matt flew out of the Seurat first. Rémy followed seconds later, his long legs splayed on landing, like Bambi ice-skating for the first time. He skidded across the hard floor, just missing the electronic security fields surrounding a small study of *A Sunday on La Grande Jatte* on the opposite wall.

Rémy looked back at the painting, which took up a full wall in the gallery. Em was pushing out of the canvas in an explosion of coloured dots, like she was fighting her way through a confetti blizzard.

Matt held his fingers to his lips. He pointed to the next gallery. Rémy nodded.

Nice work, sis. We crossed the Atlantic in about fourteen minutes. Can you handle the guard? I've got nothing left.

When the unsuspecting guard turned into the Seurat room, Em stepped in front of him.

'Hello, Bobby,' she said, scanning his badge. 'Ever wondered what it feels like to melt?'

The guard's eyes blinked rapidly for thirty seconds, his hands twitching, then Em's inspiriting hit him like a train. He collapsed to the floor in front of her, his eyes still blinking.

'Now what?' said Rémy.

'She's not done yet,' said Matt, leading Rémy to the emergency exit at the rear of the room.

Clumsily, the guard rolled to his knees and slowly stood up, eyes blinking, as if his conscious brain was fighting to regain control. Em took his hand and hustled him towards the emergency exit where Matt and Rémy were waiting.

The guard's radio clicked on. *'Bobby, check out the Seurat room, will ya? The temps just spiked in there.'*

Em's eyes opened wide. She held her hands up helplessly. She couldn't keep control of the guard's mind and make him talk at the same time.

Rémy grabbed the guard's walkie-talkie and spoke into it. 'Sure thing. On my way there now.'

Matt grinned. 'Quick thinking.'

'Not really,' said Rémy, replacing the radio on Bobby's belt. 'A lot of white people think we sound alike anyway.'

Through Em, Bobby disarmed the alarm, unlocked the door and held it open for the three of them to jump down the two stairs. Staying as close to the walls bordering the building as they could, they darted quickly between lights. With the few drops of inspiriting energy Em had left, she cracked out the camera on the corner of the building before they ran past it.

'Will the guard be OK?' whispered Rémy to Em.

'He might have a headache, and he may remember us as a wave of colour in his mind—' Em put her hand on Rémy's shoulder – 'but he'll blame it on his high blood pressure.'

The lights of Michigan Avenue spread out in front of them. Reaching to the stars, the buildings were packed like a hundred Jenga games into an incredibly small space.

'It's … it's so tall,' said Em in awe.

Despite the fact that his stomach was doing somersaults, Rémy laughed. 'I guess it is. It's sometimes called "the city with the big shoulders". Come on, I told Sotto to meet us on the next block.'

The three of them were about to run down the grassy embankment to the pavement when Matt grabbed both their arms and yanked them behind a wall. He pointed to the lions in front of the columned façade of the building.

'They're glowing,' said Rémy in surprise.

'That could have been from us when we faded inside,' said Em.

'It also might mean someone's watching this building.'

'How would anyone know we were here?'

The three of them stared at each other. Em's eyes narrowed and her jaw clenched.

'Caravaggio, the bastard!' she said. 'He comes to us for help and then he betrays us … again!'

'Or maybe the nephilim finally caught up with him,' said Matt.

'Whatever,' said Rémy. 'We can't lurk much longer in the shadows here. We're already ten minutes late.'

The traffic was trickling along Michigan Avenue. In an hour it would be streaming above them too, as the first American flight from New York banked in for a landing at Midway Airport.

'I told Sotto to meet us under the L at Wacker Drive,' Rémy told the others. 'The elevated trains we have in Chicago.'

When they turned the corner, a City of Chicago tow truck was cranking the wheels of a 1979 Cadillac up in the air. Before Matt or Em could stop him, Rémy sprinted to the truck.

'Where's the driver?' he shouted. 'What happened?'

'How the hell should I know?' snapped the truck driver. 'I just hook 'em up and get 'em to the pound.'

Em pulled Rémy back as the truck pulled into the street, with the Caddy scraping the road behind it.

'What do you think you're doing?' hissed Matt. 'We need to do this without calling attention to ourselves.'

'That was Sotto's car,' said Rémy. He pulled his arm away and sat down on the stoop of a wine bar.

Bits of rubber from the front tyres of the car were littering the kerb.

'Look at this,' said Em.

'Someone definitely knew we were coming,' Matt said.

'How can you be sure?' said Rémy. He kicked a strip of rubber with his toe, the edges pulsing in a thin blue light.

'Because,' said Em, 'an animated bullet blew out your friend's tyres.'

41.

HOME SWEET
HOME

By the time Matt, Em and Rémy reached the apartment building on foot where Rémy had spent most of his childhood, the sun was rising and traffic was heavy on the main streets. They had decided not to conjure or animate a way to get to the apartment any faster in case they were being watched. Sotto Square's building sat on a leafy tree-canopied block and housed six flats, most of them inhabited by Sotto's relatives, employees or families like Rémy's that Sotto had taken under his wing. Standing on the roof of the building and facing east, it was possible to see a sliver of Lake Michigan between the crumbling smoke-stacks and dilapidated factories that sat abandoned and empty near the shore.

An iron gate with a security pad and fence bordered the small lawn in front of the well-kept building and the parking lot and a row of garages in back. Before Rémy could punch in the code, the gate swung open. A huge black man stepped out on to the front steps, arms folded, staring at them.

Rémy half-skipped, half-jogged up the path and threw himself at the man mountain, who picked him off the ground and bear-hugged him.

'Man, I've missed you. Sotto said you was comin' for a visit.' The big man looked out at the street. 'Where's my brother at?'

'Something happened, Two,' Rémy said. 'His car was being towed from Wacker and he wasn't there.'

'Well, that doesn't sound good, does it?' Two held the outside door for the three of them. 'Best find out what's going on.'

He jogged up the stairs, surprisingly nimble for a man of his size. The others followed. The main room of the flat was comfortably furnished with the biggest suede sectional couch Em had ever seen, facing an equally giant flat screen on the opposite wall. The rooms that had once been a dining room and a bedroom were also one big space, kitted out like an executive's office with a high-back leather chair sitting behind a mahogany desk that looked museum-worthy.

'So you two must be Rémy's Irish friends,' said Two, clapping Matt and Em on the shoulder as they entered the vast space.

'Scottish,' said Em.

'Same difference, right? You sound Irish to me.'

Rémy's expression pleaded mercy from Em. She grinned and shook Two's hand. Matt did the same.

Two ushered the three of them into a recently upgraded kitchen.

'This is new,' Rémy said, running his hands over expensive marble counters. 'It used to be Sotto's bedroom.'

Two looked sidelong at Matt and Em.

'It's OK, Two. They know what happened to my mom.'

'Good. That's good,' said Two. 'Helps you get past it if you share your hurt with someone. Am I right?' he said, smiling at Em.

'You're right,' said Em, feeling a ribbon of well-meaning concern curling from Two's mind to hers.

I like this guy.

'So your mom's flat was busted up pretty bad after you both were attacked on the balcony,' Two began. 'Sotto had us mirror similar damage down here so it looked like her balcony had crashed and pulled down the entire wall and it didn't look like your balcony got singled out. Cops bought it.'

'And my ... mom?'

'We took care of her and your Tía Rosa. They're in a right nice place on Beecher. Got a tree above them and all. I can take you there, if you'd like.'

Em saw Rémy fighting back tears. She slipped her fingers into his.

'Some other time,' Rémy managed. 'Right now I really

need to get back into the apartment. I'd like to get some of my mom's things.'

'Sure. Sure.'

Two's mobile phone started vibrating in his pocket. Matt poured himself a glass of water and stared out across the balcony at the petrol station on the corner. Em followed his gaze. A flash of blue light flickered near the gas pumps. Matt shoved his shades up on to his hair and splashed water on his face.

Two handed him a towel. 'That was Sotto. He's on his way. Said not to leave the flat. Under any circumstances.'

Em was afraid of what the blue light might mean. Not leaving the flat was fine by her.

'I'll fix yous some breakfast.' Two opened a cupboard and took out a variety of bowls, and then went to the skyscraper-like refrigerator and stared inside. 'How 'bout Eggs Benedict?'

I love this guy.

42.

OVER EASY

Em and Rémy sat across from each other at a marble kitchen island big enough to land a small plane, finishing their breakfast. Two Square had left to pick up Sotto, and Matt was staring out at the petrol station again.

'Something's not right over there,' he said. 'Before breakfast I thought I saw something. Figured I was just hungry.' He shoved his shades up into his hair. 'Now I think it was an animation.'

'I saw it too,' said Em. 'Your eyes were pink just now, by the way.'

'Then we should go up to my apartment and get the painting right away, just in case we have to leave in a hurry,' said Rémy.

'You two go up to the apartment. I'll go down.' Matt looked at Rémy. 'How many entrances in this building?'

'One at the front and ... wait, give me a second.' He took out his harmonica and played the opening chords to Bob Dylan's 'All Along the Watchtower'. 'Make that just one at the front. The other one just disappeared.'

'You're getting pretty comfortable doing that,' Em observed.

'I'm gettin' pretty comfortable doing a lot of things since I met you two.'

Matt left the others on the landing and headed down the two flights to the front door, where he hid in the shadows beneath the stairs. His eyes fluttered until fragments of blue and green gilded his irises, making it possible for him to see through the front doors to the outlines of vehicles and pedestrians passing in front of the building. And he waited.

Rémy stopped dead in the hallway outside his old apartment. Em crashed into his heels. A wall of sound had hit him hard, a cacophony of high-pitched screams and banging drums with a million insects droning a bass line.

'If you want, I can fetch the painting on my own,' Em offered.

Rémy shook his head. 'I need to do this,' he said.

Using the key Two Square had given him, he pushed open the door to the apartment and moved quickly through to the kitchen.

The barrage of sound in the hallway had been bad enough, but inside it was much worse. Rémy heard the whole of his childhood playing out right where he stood. From the day he and his mom had arrived in Chicago with two suitcases and a Teen Titans lunchbox to the day he fled the city with his guitar case, a backpack and a key, music flooded his mind: classical to blues, R&B to rock to rap. Cello, violins, guitar, harmonica and beats sampling Bach, BB King, Dylan, Drake, Common and Kendrick Lamar. He collapsed into the plastic kitchen chair at the Formica table, his eyes watering, his chest tight, a thorn piercing his heart.

Standing by the kitchen door, Em felt helpless and overwhelmingly sad. She tasted pancakes and syrup, strawberries, bourbon, and chocolate ice cream. She sensed hurt and disappointment and love and pride, and something else lingering in the rooms.

Evil.

43.

WHO YOU GONNA CALL?

'You must be Matt,' said Sotto, stepping into the apartment block ahead of his younger brother who, Matt observed, was at least twice Sotto's size. Suddenly Two Square's name made sense.

Matt extended his hand, grazing Sotto's knuckles in greeting. 'There's something freaky out there so I came to check it out. We were worried that—'

'Not here.'

Sotto took the stairs two at a time.

'Go on up with him,' said Two Square, settling himself by the doors. 'I'll keep watch.'

Matt and Sotto were in the living room of the second-floor apartment before Sotto spoke again.

'Listen,' said Sotto. 'I've known for years that somethin' was different with Rém and his mom. I mean "change the world and maybe die for it" different. But it wasn't until the day Annie was murdered I knew it was fuckin' Ghostbusters different.'

'That's one way to put it,' said Matt, sitting on the edge of the massive sectional, his back to the wide windows. 'How much do you know about Rémy's particular skill set?'

'You tell me.'

Matt tried to explain Rémy's powers, how he created magic with his music.

'A Conjuror, you say? Like now-you-see-me-now-you-don't Copperfield shit? And you and your sister are the same?' said Sotto, peeling his T-shirt off as he headed down the hall towards a bathroom bursting with morning sunlight. He was both ripped and illustrated, tattoos covering his back.

'No,' said Matt, rubbing sleep from his eyes. It seemed days ago that they'd confronted the Pied Piper in Scotland, instead of only hours. 'Rémy's line is more like change-reality-with-music, Luke Cage-meets-Tempest kind of shit.'

Sotto shortly came back down the hallway after a shower, fastening his jeans and wearing a clean vintage NWA T-shirt stuck against his damp, tattooed skin. 'So does that make you and your sister the rest of the Doom Patrol?'

Matt grinned. 'We're agents for an organization called Orion. Rémy is too now, I guess.'

Sotto moved round the kitchen like a dancer, stretching for a cast-iron pan, lifting down a plate, a bowl, a whisk, reaching inside the fridge for eggs without breaking his stride. Here was a man comfortable in himself. Matt sat at the island with his sketchpad in front of him, doodling images of Sotto as he moved.

'Is Rém OK?' asked Sotto, filling a mug with coffee and handing it to Matt.

'He's upstairs with my sister.'

'Then I'll give him some time. Tough what happened. Some scary shit went down the day he left.'

Matt nodded, feeling a sharp pang of remorse for his earlier impatience with Rémy. At least he and Em had family to help smooth their way into the supernatural. Rémy hadn't been so lucky. The bad had initiated him.

'I was worried we'd been followed since we left Edinburgh and, given what happened to your car, I thought it better if I kept an eye on the street.'

Sotto whipped eggs in a bowl while a pat of butter melted on the pan. He added salt, pepper and a handful of grated cheese to the mixture. 'Outside the Art Institute, there was def' somethin',' he said, chopping a clove of garlic and some onions and tossing them into the sizzling butter. 'An' I mean somethin' not from this side of town. For a second or two, the lions looked like they were alive.'

Sotto's anxiety for Rémy hit Matt harder than his fear of what he'd witnessed. In that moment Matt recognized a trusted ally. He relaxed.

Matt quickly flipped to a page where earlier Caravaggio had sketched Luca Ferrante's likeness. He slid the pad across the island.

'His name is Luca Ferrante,' he said. 'A serious badass.'

Sotto tapped his fingers on the nephilim for a second. 'Definitely not him.' He slid the pad back. 'I saw a woman.'

In the space at the edge of the page, Matt listened to Sotto's description and sketched. Now Sotto looked interested.

'Shade her skin darker. Make her a little older.'

Matt did.

Sotto set his plate in the sink and stood at Matt's shoulder.

'Yeah,' he said. 'That looks like the bitch that shot out my tyres.'

Upstairs, Em stared at the framed photograph on the wall. Rémy in Annie's arms as a newborn, a handsome white man grinning proudly at both of them.

'That was my Tía Rosa's favourite photo of my dad,' said Rémy, coming up behind her. 'She always said he had that look of pride and awe any time he looked at both of us.' He swallowed. 'I wish he was here.'

Em set her hand on top of Rémy's, but she didn't try to lessen his hurt. She just squeezed his hand and pushed open the bedroom door.

The room smelled of Pine Sol and fresh paint. Em could detect the lingering odour of blood, but she said nothing. Despite a layer of dust on Annie's desk and the whispers of musical graffiti noticeable beneath the pale green paint, the room was immaculate. Lines of a vacuum cleaner were still visible on the carpet. Books were stacked on a birch rocking chair next to the balcony windows. Another pile was on the bedside table.

Rémy ran his hands over his head. 'I should've told Sotto not to paint the walls.'

'At least her journal's in a safe place,' said Em.

Three embroidered pillows sat against the headboard of Annie's double bed, the quilt folded with tight military corners. Rémy stared at the empty space above it.

'Yeah,' he said worriedly. 'But the painting's gone.'

44.

ON THE SAME PAGE

The alarm on the security panel next to the door buzzed. Sotto punched in a series of numbers and the door swung open.

'River City!' Sotto kissed the top of Rémy's head. 'For 'while we was thinkin' you got left.'

'Nah,' said Rémy, grinning. 'Still here.'

'River City?' asked Em.

'The Music Man?' said Sotto, squeezing Rémy's shoulders. 'Trouble in River City?'

Rémy laughed. 'He's called me that since we moved here.' A flash outside the window like a mirror reflecting the sun caught his eye. He blinked, shook his head. 'And thanks,' he added. 'For ... you know. Taking care of my mom.'

'The police kept her for a while, but when the case went cold...' Sotto shrugged. 'We know you would've done the same for us.'

The light flashed again.

'Did you see that?' Em asked Matt, who shook his head.

'I need your help again, Sotto,' said Rémy. 'What happened to the painting of the angel playing the violin that was above my mom's bed?'

Four tear-gas canisters burst through the window at once, shattering the glass before exploding in the middle of the room. Glass rained down. Em screamed as the air filled with thick, choking fog.

'Five O!' hollered Two, charging through the front door.

Sotto tapped his watch. The door slammed behind Two, sealing with a *whoosh*. It was clear that they had done this before.

'Masks!' Sotto shouted.

Everyone ran for the back rooms of the apartment, trying to get away from the gas. Matt was scribbling as fast as he was moving. Two threw open a cupboard on the way and grabbed two army gas masks hanging inside the door. In the same instant, two masks dropped from a crack of light above Matt, who tossed one to Em and pulled the other over his own head.

'At least we're on the same page,' said Sotto, as everyone fastened the masks to their faces.

They sprinted for the bedroom. Sotto slammed the door. Gas insinuated itself into the room like warm breath on a frigid day. They all heard a loud banging on the apartment's front door.

'In here.'

Sotto guided everyone into what looked like a walk-in closet, but wasn't.

'Whoa,' said Rémy, looking around at the safe room with its flat-screen security camera mounted in the middle of a wall of first-edition mysteries, all sealed in Plexiglas containers.

Sotto slammed the steel-encased door. It, too, sealed with a *whoosh*. 'Should be safe in here,' he said.

Everyone took off their masks. Em ran shaky fingers over the hard spines on the first editions. On the security monitor they could see what looked like two Chicago SWAT officers in full masked gear at the apartment door. One of the officers was kneeling and holding an electronic pick at the lock.

'Not Five O,' said Two. His eyes were bloodshot and the skin beneath them beginning to puff like bread dough.

'Oh my God,' gasped Em. 'Two, you didn't get a mask.'

Two shrugged off the problem and pointed at the screen. 'If they find Rémy, they'll kill him. I'll call their bluff and stall.'

He opened the safe-room door and ran back into the choking fog. On the flat-screen, they watched him kneel on the living-room floor and lock his hands behind his head.

'That's gotta hurt,' said Matt, with feeling.

Sotto reached under a shelf, exposing a security pad. He placed two fingers on it and pressed. Up on the ceiling the dome light shifted to the left, the faux ceiling slid away, and a folded ladder dropped out of the space.

'It's not magic,' Em said to Sotto, 'but it's pretty cool.'

They all heard a pneumatic drill start up, tearing through the steel front door. Sotto checked the screen.

'Where did that come from?' he said. 'They didn't have no drill last time I looked.'

'From him,' said Matt.

He pointed to a third person standing slightly off camera, dressed in a single-breasted camel coat and skinny black trousers, and holding a sketchpad open in his hand.

'That's the pedestrian I saw earlier at the Art Institute,' said Sotto. 'Is it your Ferrante guy?'

'According to our source, Luca Ferrante is tall, muscular, older,' said Em. 'This guy is younger and skinnier.'

The drill was getting louder, high-pitched, screaming. On the security panels, they could see the newcomer slide the pad into his coat pocket and back up into the shadows.

'He's got skills,' said Sotto. 'He knows where the cameras are hidden, and I hid them babies good.'

Em kept her eyes on the screen while Matt helped Sotto unfold the last section of the ladder.

'Why would an Animare not just blow open the door?' she asked, puzzled. 'Make it disappear even? Why go to all the trouble of creating a drill?'

'I'm OK with it,' said Sotto. 'It's slowing them down, givin' us more time to get out.'

45.

IN THE
CLOSET

Rémy was only half-listening to Matt and Em's debate. Mostly he was thinking about Two, exposed and vulnerable in the living room, taking a hit for him. Again.

'Is Two gonna be OK?'

'He knows the drill,' replied Sotto, climbing on to the ladder.

There was no way Rémy was leaving another situation for Two to clean up. He inhaled deeply, pulled up his mask and tugged open the door.

'No!' shouted Sotto. 'Two can handle it.'

It was the reflection from the mirror in the bathroom on the far side of the bedroom that changed Rémy's mind. *Rest on the Flight into Egypt* was hanging above Sotto's spa tub. He ran to the bathroom, lifted the painting from the wall and sprinted back.

'Are you crazy?' demanded Sotto, slamming the door

again. 'These guys want you bad. Are you just going to hand yourself over?'

Rémy set the painting against the wall of books. Its heavy frame was shining, the gilt gleaming from a recent polish. It was all he could do not to collapse on to the floor and give up. His whole life, this had been above his mom's bed. His whole life she had been protecting it, protecting him.

'They want this more,' he said aloud. 'What was it doing in your bathroom?'

'Figured it was as safe a place as any.'

Sotto reactivated the seal on the door, and a ventilation fan sucked out the eye-watering gas that had penetrated the space. The drilling sound on the front door was muffled, but clearly audible through the walls.

'They'll be through that door in a sec,' Matt said.

Em's eyes traced the glow around the edges of Caravaggio's model angel, his elaborately detailed wings, and the shimmer from the sheet music of the Devil's Interval held reverently in Joseph's hand.

'It made me feel when I looked at it,' said Sotto, his hands in his pockets, his head tilted at the painting. 'I guess that's why I brought it down to the flat.'

'Art will do that,' said Em. 'If you let it.'

Behind his sister, Matt was drawing something. Em threw up her hand, catching the handle of an X-Acto blade that flashed into reality above her as Matt closed his pad. She kneeled and swiftly sliced into the canvas, cutting a tight clean line as close under the frame as she could.

'My mom stole this painting a long time ago,' explained Rémy to Sotto, as Em rolled the canvas up. 'The Camarilla – the guys who killed Mom and Tía Rosa – and Luca Ferrante, they want it back. Badly. It's part of a bigger plan. An apocalyptic plan.'

'So this Camarilla want you too?' asked Sotto. 'And Ferrante's calling the shots?'

Rémy nodded.

'Good to know,' said Sotto, as if he'd been told the price of eggs had gone up.

Outside, the pneumatic drill was hiccupping, making its final cuts in the front door.

'We should be out there,' Rémy said in frustration. 'Helping. Two's not going to hold them for long.'

'No,' said Matt, heading up the ladder. 'We need to get this painting back to Orion. Two'll be OK.'

Em rolled the canvas and slipped it inside Rémy's jacket. She glanced at Matt and Sotto and the safe-room door, then back at Rémy.

'Do it!' she said.

Rémy yanked open the door and stepped back into the bedroom. He needed to conjure something to slow down the intruders. He dropped his mask to his neck and put his harmonica to his lips, playing lightly at first, and then with a fervour that rang with the full force of his imagination.

'We gotta bail right now, River City,' said Sotto, his foot on the first rung, his eyes on the security panel.

'Almost there.'

Rémy ignored the searing pain in his throat and the burning in his eyes as he conjured to Lightnin' Hopkins' 'Fugitive Blues'. The wood planks on the hall floor snapped up one after the other and shot into the hallway below like torpedoes, leaving a dangerous gaping hole like a moat.

46.

NO SMOKING

Rémy and Matt pulled the ladder up into the crawl space. Below them the faux ceiling slid back into place.

'I added this after the attack on your mom,' said Sotto.

Hunched over but moving fast, he led them along a reinforced air duct the width of the building which ran between his apartment and Rémy's above. They climbed up a rope ladder and on to a scaffold beneath a skylight. Sotto popped the lock, sliding the skylight open.

'Wait,' said Em. 'Something's not right. My skin is tingling.'

Sotto looked at her. 'No kidding.'

'Hear her out, man,' said Rémy. 'Em can feel stuff you really want to know about.'

'I saw a weird flash of light outside the window before those canisters were tossed,' Em said. 'There's something else out there. Something bad.'

'Maybe the bitch that shot out my tyres,' said Sotto.

Matt filled Em and Rémy in on his and Sotto's conversation in the kitchen. The daylight coming through the skylight illuminated the small space.

'Can we maybe get outside first and then figure out what's going on?' Matt suggested.

'No,' said Sotto, climbing out. 'Stay there until I see what's goin' down.'

Matt shouldered his way through the skylight after him. Sotto glared.

'If something isn't right, I can help,' Matt said. He tapped his sketchpad in the pocket inside his jacket. 'Fastest draw in the west, remember?' He glanced back at Rémy. 'Get Em to put the painting in something more secure than your jacket, man.'

Rémy and Em watched Sotto and Matt back away from the skylight, their footsteps soon lost in the distance. The tingling was like burning goosebumps on Em's scalp. She realized she was trembling.

Rémy leaned close to her, his harmonica gripped in his hand. 'Are you OK?'

'Just the damp and the dark,' Em said, trying to ignore how her stomach was cramping. 'Maybe I'm getting sick.'

'Can your kind get sick?'

'We're Animare, not aliens.' Em scratched her scalp aggressively before she dug her sketchbook out and, with broad thick strokes, drew an airtight aluminium poster tube for the painting.

Rémy slid his arm round Em's waist, pulling her closer. 'You feel warm,' he said.

Em glanced round at the narrow scaffold platform they were sitting on. 'Just a little anxious in this tight space.'

Rémy rolled the canvas inside the tube and sealed the top before slipping it inside his jacket sleeve. Em leaned into him and yawned.

'So now we have the Conjuror and the sacred chord,' she said, exhaustion seeping through her words. 'Let's go home. Caravaggio can destroy this and the Camarilla will stop chasing you.'

'I love your optimism,' said Rémy, tightening his embrace. 'But why not destroy it now?'

'Because I'm not destroying a priceless work of art on Caravaggio's word alone. Let's get it back to Orion first and run a few more checks.'

'You know you're scratching your head a lot?'

Em shot upright, her fingernails tearing at the skin on her scalp.

'Do you smell that?'

'What?'

'Smoke.'

'I don't smell anything.'

'I can taste ash in my mouth.' Em spat off the edge of the scaffold. Both hands were clawing at her scalp, her nails drawing blood.

'You're freaking me out now,' said Rémy. 'Whether Sotto likes it or not, we need to get out of here.'

He reached for the skylight. Em let out an awful scream and threw herself to the ground, rolling back and forth.

'My hair's on fire. My head. Aaargh!'

Rémy lunged on top of her and grabbed her wrists. 'Look at me.'

Wide-eyed with terror, Em stared into Rémy's eyes, fighting against his grip.

'Your hair is not on fire. Something is doing this to you.'

Em bucked and wrestled. Her body was convulsing violently and she was reeling towards the edge of the platform.

'Em!' Rémy shouted. 'You're going to—'

It wasn't far from the scaffold platform to the ground, but it was far enough. As she fell, Em hit her head on a beam with a sickening crack. For a moment, everything went black.

'Shit!' Rémy had scrambled down the rope ladder beside her. 'Talk to me!'

Em forced her eyes open against the pain in her head. 'My scalp hurts so much, please make it stop...'

Rémy played a fast riff on his harmonica and caught the flashlight before it clattered out of sight. He put it in his mouth. With his hand gripping Em's wrists, he held her steady enough to aim the light at her scalp. He gasped. The torch clattered to the ground.

'What's wrong?' Em gasped, gripped with terror. 'What can you see?'

47.

NOT GONNA LIE

A circle of wet red welts was erupting on Em's crown. Thin writhing snakes stabbed through the sores, like she was Medusa. Rémy wrapped his arms more tightly round her to stop her from tearing at the grotesque eruption on her head.

'It's bad,' he said, swallowing. 'Not gonna lie. But we're gonna fix it, OK?'

He held his harmonica to his lips with some difficulty. What did you conjure to stop such horror? His mind was blank.

Em closed her eyes. The snakes began to calm down, settling, no longer snapping at one another. Rémy realized that Em was inspiriting herself, quieting her body and mind.

'Good,' said Rémy, tightening his embrace as the snakes became more lethargic. 'That's good. Keep doing what you're doing...'

Holding Em there in the darkness, Rémy's anguish

played in his mind like a lone cello. The longer he sat with her, the louder and fuller the music became. No longer a lone lament, but a requiem. He just had to make sure it wasn't for his friends. They had all sacrificed so much for him.

Leaning close, he whispered, 'I need you to do something important for me.'

Em nodded almost imperceptibly.

'Send a message to Matt. With your mind. Tell him and Sotto to meet us at the Art Institute. Tell him not to come back up here.'

An angry wound erupted through Em's skin, her heart beating like a hummingbird against Rémy's chest.

'Please,' said Rémy. 'I know it's hard.'

In his head, Rémy heard the echoes of Em's voice. All her pain, her horror, and her hold on this reality sounded like a million fingernails on a chalkboard. And then he heard nothing and she went limp in his arms.

He kissed her cheek and set her down gently, making sure that she was comfortable. Using the flashlight, he found her sketchpad and charcoal crayon. When he'd finished writing, he tore out the page, folded it and stuck it under the collar of her T-shirt.

Making sure the aluminium tube with the canvas was safely inside the sleeve of Em's coat, he climbed up on the scaffold and jumped through the skylight. He sprinted to the edge and jumped, landing hard on the new balcony outside his mom's old bedroom. Ignoring the pain in his knee, he ran through his apartment to his Tía Rosa's bedroom, where he lifted the only piece of art she'd ever had on her wall and unceremoniously tore it out of its frame. Then he sprinted downstairs.

Halfway down the stairwell, he stopped. He could hear voices: a man and a woman, arguing. He put his harmonica to his lips and, with as little sound as possible, began conjuring.

At first he thought his exhaustion and anxiety were blocking his imagination, but after a second chord progression a spiral of sound swirled above his head. An aluminium tube twice as big as the one he'd just tucked inside Em's sleeve bounced from the mist, hitting Rémy's shoulder. He lunged and caught it before it clattered on the stairs. Then he rolled the canvas from Tía Rosa's bedroom, dropped it inside the container and closed it. Just one more thing to conjure.

When his conjuring was complete, he slid his harmonica into his jacket pocket. With the new container tucked under his arm, he crept out of the stairwell.

Sotto's front door looked as if it had been opened with a can opener. The voices were louder here. Rémy flattened his back against the wall next to the door and exhaled slowly. Then, holding the heavy tube in front of his chest, he walked into Sotto's apartment.

48.

THE MAN IN THE CAMEL COAT

The first thing Rémy saw was Two on the ground, red bulges for eyes, his hands and his feet bound with plastic cuffs. He was unconscious, but breathing. That was some relief anyway. Under the guise of feeling for a pulse, Rémy slipped the second note he'd written inside his friend's shirt.

He faced the man in the camel coat, who was reclining in the centre of Sotto's massive U-shaped sectional couch. They locked eyes, before the man nodded at something behind Rémy's shoulder.

Rémy pivoted and ducked a second too late. A baton smashed against the side of his head, splitting his earlobe and sending shudders of pain along his jaw. The blow was enough to knock him down, but not enough to knock him out. As he collapsed, he dropped the aluminium tube, which rolled across the floor to the feet of the man on the couch.

Blood trickled from Rémy's ear towards the Conjuror's mark. A rush of adrenaline fuelled his senses, making him aware of every sound in the building. The creaking of the neighbours on the other side of the hallway, the traffic on the street outside, the tick of a clock in the kitchen, the deep but anxious breathing of the man in the camel coat.

In any other circumstances, this surge of energy would have fuelled his powers. He would have slipped his harmonica from his pocket and conjured the man face-first through the shattered window on to the pavement outside. But conjuring to save himself would defeat the purpose of why he'd strolled into the apartment in the first place.

Groaning, Rémy rolled on to his back and looked up at his attacker, a middle-aged black dude with a boxer's nose and a flat chin. The man was grinning and slapping the baton against his palm, ready for another blow.

The man in the camel coat signalled for him to back off.

'That was too easy, boss,' said the attacker in a Chicago accent, jabbing at Rémy's throat with the baton, exposing the black ink of the Camarilla tattooed on his wrist.

'You have me and you have the canvas,' croaked Rémy, pulling himself to his knees. 'But I'm willing to offer you more.'

Up close, the boss was younger than Rémy had first thought. Twenty something, maybe. He was white, but he'd been in the sun recently and a spray of freckles covered the bridge of his nose. His hair was slick with product and swept off his lean, chiselled face. He wore an earring, a black stone about the size of a tiny pebble with something etched on it that Rémy couldn't make out. He was built like an athlete, and easily as tall as Rémy. His boots were black, with silver pointed tips, his eyes cold and calculating. Rémy wondered, with a twist in his gut, if this guy was already two moves ahead of him.

He slid his hand inside his jacket pocket.

'I'll trade you my conjuring powers to use as you want,' he said as evenly as he could, 'but only if you leave my friends alone. Forever. If I hear that they are in danger, or worse, I will destroy you all with one note, the way I destroyed the last guy you sent to find me. You know a Conjuror is the only one who can stop your plans. But you also know I'm the only one who can make the Second Kingdom a reality. I am the Camarilla's worst nightmare and its greatest hope.'

He held out his harmonica. The man in the camel coat took it. Then he opened the top of the aluminium tube and glanced inside.

'It's the one you're looking for,' said Rémy, his pulse quickening. 'The one with the Devil's Interval.'

Rémy thought he saw a flash of compassion flit across the man's face, but it was short-lived. He flicked his hand and his henchman was on Rémy again, his rough hands on his neck, squeezing the air from his lungs.

Rémy's anger surged. He kicked backwards, the heel of his boot nailing the attacker's shin. Rémy heard the bone snap. He bent his arm, punched his elbow into the man's windpipe, and watched with satisfaction when he face-planted on the hardwood floor. *That was for Two,* Rémy thought, *and Sotto and Em and my mom and Tía Rosa.*

Rémy regained his balance and his breath, but not fast enough. The man in the camel coat was gently pressing a stiletto blade against Two's neck, blood oozing around its tip, and regarding him curiously.

'Don't kill him,' said Rémy, raising his hands in surrender. 'Who are you?'

Ignoring the question, the man removed a silver clip of dollar bills from the front of his jeans. He dropped half the money on his unconscious henchman and handed the rest to a second man, who had remained standing at the kitchen archway without intervening in the fight. For a second Rémy wondered if everything that had happened so far had all been an elaborate ruse.

Had he been played?

Before he had time to formulate an answer, a syringe stabbed his thigh. Rémy heaved a sigh and slid to the ground.

49.

IN HER WAKE

Em was in the swimming pool at the Abbey, propelling herself towards the blue tiled edge. She tucked, flipped, and launched off the wall at least one full stroke before Zach hit his turn in the lane next to her. Without thinking, she grinned, swallowed water, chopped her stroke, and gave Zach the extra seconds he needed to pull up beside her.

She glanced at his eyes, which were smiling beneath his goggles, and kicked harder, pulling long and deep. One stroke, two, three. Zach was right there, tight on her lane marker, using her wake. Almost at the wall, she speeded up her rotation, shoulders burning, legs like jelly. Zach was dropping back again. At the wall, she turned, kicking three times before stroking the surface.

When she rose to breathe, she was no longer in the Abbey's pool. The walls in this place were mosaic tiles in broken and cracked reds, yellows and burnished blues.

The ceiling was a barrel-vaulted arch. The water was no longer cold. Instead it was bubbling. Steaming.

Burning.

Em tried to make her limbs move, but they wouldn't obey. Her body spasmed, her skin blistering, peeling into the pool. Then she wasn't in water any more. She was wading neck-deep in snakes writhing and squirming over her body, wrapping around her neck, choking her.

Zach was standing on the edge of this strange cracked pool, his body dripping with big beads of water that shimmered in the light. He was waving. Em wanted to wave back but she couldn't.

A snake crawled across her face. Then another, this one with two heads. Her heart was heavy, her chest tightening. She stared again at Zach.

He was still waving furiously.

50.

FIRST AID

Two Square dribbled more water on Em's face. The rest he held to her lips to drink. She gulped, coughing and choking as she swallowed.

'Easy. Easy there.'

'What happened?' rasped Em, her head lolling against Two's chest. 'Where's Rémy?'

'Later,' he said. 'We need to get you to the Art Institute now.'

He lifted Em over his shoulder like she was a feather and climbed the rope ladder to the top of the scaffold, before heaving her out through the skylight and on to the roof. He pulled himself up and out after her. The sun was bright. He cupped his hands around his bloodshot, stinging eyes, trying to adjust his focus. He couldn't see anything down on the tree-lined street.

At his feet, Em moaned. Two pulled a Cubs baseball cap from his back pocket and was about to pull it over her distinctive pink streaked hair when the raw blistering burns on her scalp stopped him. He was pretty sure burns should be left uncovered. She was shivering, he saw, mostly likely from shock. He knew the symptoms. He'd learned more than how to disable a bomb after two tours in Iraq.

At edge of the roof, he jumped down, like a large, lithe cat on to one of Sotto's side balconies. He pressed his hand on the glass at the handle, and waited for his palm print to glow yellow. The door slid open silently. Seconds later he climbed back up to the roof with a fur throw from his bed, set Em in the middle, and swaddled her up.

Em moaned again. Two set her over his shoulder and climbed nimbly down the fire escape at the back of the apartment building. At the bottom, he paused for a minute. He had a decision to make. Should he get Em to the Art Institute as instructed, or take her back inside, call a doctor?

He was a soldier. He followed orders.

He stepped quickly to the front of the building, staying under the cover of the trees, marched to the front gate, and looked along the street.

What did you conjure for us, eh, River City? What?

At the end of the block, he spotted a pink mini-van he'd never seen before. It was completely out of place. Unmissable.

Jeez. You're killin' me here, Rém.

Two jogged to the van. The keys were in the ignition. He adjusted the mirror, and then noticed a wheelchair in the back. After settling Em in the bench seat, he called Sotto.

'You OK?'

Two pulled out and headed towards the loop. 'I'm fine. The girl, not so much.'

'What?'

Two slowed to a stop at the next intersection. A Chicago cop pulled up next to him, tapped his ear and signalled to Two to put down his phone.

Two heaved a sigh. 'Gotta go, bro. We'll be there in ten.'

51.

TIME TRANSFIXED

nside the small gallery at the Art Institute, Matt paced in front of the Seurat, waiting for Em and Rémy to show. He could still hear how faint Em's voice had been in his mind.

Art Institute. Meet us there.

It had been hard to hear her. And he hadn't heard her since.

Two guards in the gallery were watching him keenly. He knew he looked like a homeless teenager. His jacket was ripped and his T-shirt ancient to begin with, and his hair was curly and wild and hanging over his face. On top of that he could not remove his shades. His eyes were flipping colour every few seconds. He was afraid that if he stood still and focused for even a second, his croc-eyes would kick in. He really didn't need the distraction of Native American wars, factory riots or gangsters, which were the only things he knew about Chicago. Em knew more.

Em.

Where are you?

His question sounded hollow in his head, echoing across a ravine to nowhere.

Sotto beckoned him over from the bench in the middle of the gallery. 'Two's on his way,' he said.

'And Em?' Matt asked, almost afraid to hear the answer.

'She's with him.'

Relief washed through Matt. 'What about Rémy?'

'Don't know. Two will fill us in.'

Matt forced a smile at the hovering guards. He and Sotto wandered through two more galleries, killing time. Sotto kept texting and Matt kept looking over his shoulder for Em, or anything or anyone glowing. He was working hard to keep panic at bay.

They stopped in front of Magritte's *Time Transfixed*.

'I always liked this one,' said Sotto. 'The train coming through the fireplace, the clock on the mantel. G'ma would bring Two and me in here on her days off. Kept us off the streets.'

'Didn't really work, did it?' said Matt unthinkingly. 'You may live in a fancy apartment, but you still make your money illegally.'

Sotto's anger hit him like a punch. Came from nowhere and then it was gone.

'Dude,' Sotto said, poking Matt's chest with his finger. 'You don't get to judge me or my family. You don't get to know what I've had to do to survive.'

'I'm sorry,' Matt muttered after a moment. 'I'm just angry. I shouldn't have left Em and Rémy behind on the roof.'

'We're all angry, man,' said Sotto. 'It's about the focus.'

The guards had changed in the gallery, making it possible for Matt and Sotto to sit by the Seurat again and watch the entrance.

'You'll 'preciate this,' said Sotto, looking up from his phone. 'Two SWAT cops were found by that gas station on my block a little while back. They have no memory of what happened. Said they stopped at the 7/11 and next thing their coffees were cold and they both had massive headaches. Do you think it has somethin' to do with that light you saw earlier? With the cops who broke into my place?'

'They were inspirited,' said Matt, resting his arms on his legs. 'Hypnotized. The camel-coat guy must have used their uniforms for his own guys. Which makes him a Guardian, I guess. Although I still can't figure out where he got that drill.'

'A Guardian is different from you, right?' said Sotto. 'You're an Aminus or something.'

'Animare,' said Matt. 'We draw things into life and we can move in and out of art. Guardians can't animate, but they can control minds and emotions. We're supposed to work together: a Guardian keeping an Animare safe, an Animare keeping a Guardian on their toes.'

'So you and your sister are Animare.'

'It's not as simple as that,' said Matt. 'We're hybrids. The only ones in existence. Half-Animare, half-Guardian. Thanks to our parents marrying illegally and having us, we can draw and control emotions and minds. Em's particularly strong in that area. No one likes Animare with mind control, or Guardians who can animate. Too much power, all in one place. We break the rules.'

'Join the club,' said Sotto. 'Dad was Puerto Rican. Mom was black from Milwaukee.'

'If the camel-coat guy is a Guardian,' said Matt, 'he must have had an Animare with him to draw the drill into life. I saw the sketchpad they used. Although I swear there were only three of them outside that door earlier. Him and the two inspirited SWAT guys.'

'Maybe the camel-coat guy is another hybrid,' said Sotto.

Matt shook his head. Almost laughed. 'We're the only ones out there with dual powers.'

'But what if you're not?'

Sotto's suggestion sent an arrow to Matt's brain, pinging an alarm.

'In my world, for centuries people passed as white who were black,' Sotto went on with a shrug. 'Why not in yours? What if this Ferrante guy has a hybrid like you and your sister at his beck and call?'

Matt ran his hands through his hair. It made perfect sense. He and Em were still confronting a culture of disdain and disbelief. Even Orion kept them on a probationary status, using their powers when it suited, but refusing them full access to the Councils and their knowledge. Of course, if you were a hybrid, you'd claim to be one or the other. A Guardian or an Animare. You would try to pass.

Wouldn't you?

52.

SNAKES ON
THE BRAIN

Matt left the Seurat. He walked into another gallery and stood in front of a Kandinsky that reflected much more how he was feeling. What if everything he had ever thought turned out not to be true? What if there really was another hybrid out there, another freak like him and Em, working for Luca and the Camarilla?

He heard a squeaking behind him and turned fast. A wheelchair rammed into his legs.

'Em!' He kneeled next to her, taking her hand. 'Are you OK?'

Em was slouched in the wheelchair, a lopsided grin on her pale face, her matted hair plastered to her scalp. 'No,' she said. 'But thanks to Rémy and Two here, I'm not dead, so there's that.'

Em tilted her head, revealing the injuries to her scalp. Matt turned white.

'One minute, my scalp was tingling,' Em said. 'And the next, snakes were tearing through my brain. I don't remember much after that.'

'Probably good that you don't,' said Two, his beefy hands gripping the arms of the wheelchair.

'Jesus,' said Matt. 'Snakes?'

Sotto hit the button for the cafeteria at the elevators. No one spoke until they reached the counter, where they ordered Coke and lattes.

'Where's Rémy?' asked Sotto as they sat at a table by the window.

Two shrugged and picked at the small puncture wound at his neck. 'He was gone before I came to. Don't know what happened to him.'

'He left this note.' Em pulled out the torn page and handed it to Matt.

'He left me one too,' said Two.

Em read hers first.

My family died protecting me. I never had friends before you two. But I can't let you fight my battles. I will use myself as bait and stop the Camarilla when I get close.
I will end this on my own. Go back to Scotland. Be safe.

Love Rémy

Two unfolded his note.

Em's in the roof. She's hurt. Get her to the
Art Institute fast. Love you both. I may not
see you again. Thanks for being my brothers.

River City

'Damn fool,' said Sotto, slapping the table.

'Em,' said Matt. 'Can you remember what paintings here other than the Seurat have exits?'

Em leaned back in the wheelchair and closed her eyes. 'None of the European works here have one. We need to find something by an American Animare.'

'What about Jacob Lawrence?' Sotto suggested. 'Two of my favourites are on loan here.'

They left the cafeteria the same way they came in. With Sotto in the lead, they breezed through a series of galleries until they reached the gallery of modern American art.

The Jacob Lawrence was glorious. It had energy and brilliant colours, and a crowd of African-American men and women in chunky cubist design marching across a bridge towards a rabid angry wolf.

'It's about standing up,' said Sotto. 'The wolf was slavery, but it could be anythin'.'

'It's stunning,' said Matt, gazing at the painting. 'But it isn't going to work. We need a painting with another painting inside it. That's how we can travel, you see.'

'What about *The Visitors*?' Sotto nodded at a second Lawrence painting.

As soon as Matt looked at *The Visitors*, he knew it would work. But where it would take them, he had no idea. The painting was of a parlour filled with guests, family members of the sick person in the bed visible through the bedroom door in the background. In the bedroom below a window depicted the skyline of Harlem. Matt could see the telltale glow of an exit painting resting behind the bed.

'Help me with Em,' said Matt, pulling his pad from his jacket pocket.

Two scooped Em from the chair. Matt enveloped his sister in his arms.

'Em, I need you to put your legs round my waist,' he instructed.

Em's head flopped against his shoulder. Matt felt her pain wash over him, and something else was wrapped inside it. Terror. A long aluminium tube pressed against his neck.

'Is that Caravaggio's canvas?' he asked.

Em was too exhausted to speak aloud. *It's safe for now,* she whispered in Matt's mind.

The suspicious guards were back.

'You better get moving,' said Two.

'Do what you got to. And then find our boy,' said Sotto, resting his hand on Matt's shoulder.

Matt nodded at Two. 'Thanks for getting her back here. And I'm sorry, but we need to ask you one more thing.'

★

There was a terrible commotion in the gallery minutes later. Two heaved a gasp and collapsed on the floor blocking the entrance to the gallery, his body twitching, drool running to his chin.

'Call 911!' yelled Sotto, skidding across the floor to his brother's side and ripping open Two's jacket and shirt as if about to start CPR. 'He's having a heart attack.'

The guards swarmed from the closest galleries, walkie-talkies squawking, kneeling next to Sotto. A crowd gathered, standing off at a polite distance, phones out. Two rolled his eyes back in his head, but not before noting how Matt and Em's bodies paled and shrank, or how two thick black arms were stretching out from the painting, wrapping themselves round the siblings and drawing them into the green-and-purple parlour.

FOURTH MOVEMENT

'Come forth ... so the chosen
shall inherit the earth.'

Book of Songs

53.

THROUGH THE
LOOKING GLASS

The arms belonged to an elderly black man in a white shirt, black tie and a grey waistcoat. A black woman in a red apron, eating cake at a yellow table, smiled warmly at Matt and Em as they surged past her in a frisson of light.

An immaculately coiffed woman stood up from a couch. 'Oh, my,' she said, her pearl earrings like tiny strobe lights winking every time she moved her head. 'Put that poor child on the sofa. Jefferson, move.'

Jefferson moved. Matt carried a dazed Em to the couch, where the woman pulled a yellow-and-red tasselled blanket over her. Matt inhaled deeply, his hands trembling. It had been a while since he'd faded without Em's help. His eyelids were fluttering like a wasp's wings, distorting his vision so that he was seeing this world through a shattered lens set on a green filter.

'You'd better sit too, boy,' said the older man in the

waistcoat, offering his wooden chair next to the kitchen door. 'You look bushed. The name's August.' He nodded towards the woman in the pearl earrings. 'My daughter, Evie. Her husband, Jefferson. That's Brother Paul on the chair. My youngest, Ella, with baby Franklin. My sister, Flo, is in the kitchen and Reverend Gaines is with Ambuya, our mother.' He looked into Matt's kaleidoscope eyes. 'You're welcome here.'

'The Calder twins,' said Brother Paul, crossing his legs, his accent a lilting southern drawl. 'Heard 'bout y'all.'

'Good things, I hope,' said Matt nervously.

'Depends,' he said, his stare focused and penetrating. 'What y'all gonna do 'bout Rémy?'

Matt's eyes finally stilled. 'You know about Rémy?'

'You think y'all the only ones with secrets and ways to share them?' said Brother Paul, looking down his long nose at Matt.

Matt wasn't sure if he meant Animare, white people or people outside this painted space. 'I need a safe place to let my sister rest while I get help for her and for Rémy. He appears to have gone off on his own.'

'To do what?' asked August, the man in the waistcoat.

'He thinks he can stop the Camarilla by himself,' said Matt.

'Stop the rise of the Second Kingdom, you mean,' said Brother Paul.

So they knew about the Second Kingdom too. Matt nodded.

'Can he?' said Evie, straightening her red shawl over her thin shoulders. 'Stop the rising evil by himself?'

'Honestly?' said Matt, tugging his shades from his hair and slipping them on. 'I doubt it. Not on his own.'

'Come to me,' said a quiet voice from the brass bed in the background of the painted space.

Matt stood at the side of the bed. He was facing a skinny minister who was comforting its elderly occupant. A slash of white paint marked the minister's collar, in stark contrast to his featureless face, where his expression was simply a series of thick strokes of black paint.

The old woman in the bed had eyes like black marbles and her face was scarred at the hinges of her chapped lips. She was horrible and beautiful at the same time. Matt perched cautiously on the edge of the bed. She crooked her finger. He leaned closer. She smelled of eucalyptus and warm bread.

'The first Conjuror came to us in a slave ship,' Ambuya whispered. Her words were slurred, but they dripped with defiance. 'He made the ultimate sacrifice so that your world could remain in balance.'

Her hand shot out from under her red blanket and grabbed Matt's. Her fingers were skeletal, her skin like tissue paper over her bones, but her grip was strong. She squeezed his hand and hope shot up his arm. His scalp tingled, and his eyes fluttered furiously for a second until his vision corrected so that it was close to normal sight, or as close as it ever was. He felt more awake than he had all day.

'Leave your sister with us,' said the old woman. 'She'll be safe till your return. Use the mirror. It'll take you where you imagine you need to be.'

'The mirror?' Matt had never heard of using anything other than a painting as a way to fade.

'Y'all don't get to have everything,' she said, accepting a sip of iced water from the faceless minister.

Set in an elegant green frame, the mirror was as purple as the thick carpet and the high-backed velvet chair from which Brother Paul continued to watch Matt suspiciously. It hung between two candelabra shaped like tree branches, and for the first time Matt noticed the way that it matched a mirror on the old woman's nightstand.

He looked down at his sister on the couch. *I'll be back with help, Em.*

What about the painting?

It's safer with you than with me. I'm not sure where I'm going to end up.

Be careful. I love you, Mattie.

Ella shifted baby Franklin to one side and moved away from the mirror. Matt stared into its swirling purple and began to sketch with frenzied, focused strokes.

54.

A DISTURBING DARKNESS

Rémy heard the music first. Someone near him was playing a violin off-key, the chords dissonant and despairing. Disoriented, groggy and with dread weighing heavy on his chest, he opened his eyes.

The darkness around him was beyond anything he'd experienced before. It had mass. It had a smell. Like syrup on his eyelids. Like wet dog and blood and shit and ripe fruit and turpentine.

Where the hell was he?

His body felt pummelled, but inside his head was light and airy, disconnected from reality. Like the way he'd felt after getting his tonsils removed, or when he'd smoked weed with Sotto on his balcony in Chicago. Warily, he forced himself to sit still for a minute, breathing through his mouth until his eyes adjusted to the gloom. His hands were numb, pinned under him as if he'd been unceremoniously dumped beneath...

Beneath a tree.

His eyes were adjusting. A gust of decay blew through the foliage. Bile churned in his gut. Rémy tried to shake his hands to get the circulation back, but he could hardly move them. With great difficulty, he pulled himself upright. Like he was wearing a lead apron, the pressure on his chest worsening. He could hear music.

Taking shallow breaths to settle his stomach, he followed the music to a spot in the thick foliage where a beautiful young woman in a pale pink shift stood playing. She smiled at Rémy, before her expression turned sorrowful and she stared away into the trees. Her playing became more agitated and her music more alarming. Rémy followed her gaze.

Three unclothed creatures with thick animal haunches were skinning a satyr, part-man, part-beast. The hind legs of the satyr were those of a hairy black goat, and his upper body was covered in similar thick black fur. He was alive, hanging upside down by his hooves from the canopy of trees, his human mouth gaping in a silent scream. The violin's high-pitched chords gave the horror its voice. His naked veins pulsed his blood into a bucket set beneath him, where a wild dog lapped it up.

Rémy was moving in slow motion. Like invisible weights were attached to his arms and his legs. Like he was fighting gravity. Like he was bound in a painting.

His mouth opened in a scream to match the satyr's. No sound came out.

55.

TOO FAR OUT

Inside painted space, time is either ephemeral or eternal. To know which, one must fade in and out of the art, as Caravaggio had over the centuries. But Em had never been in this kind of stasis for more than an hour or two, and she was worried. What if Matt didn't find his way back to Orion and the church? What if she was bound here for ever? She stressed about the painting hidden in her sleeve. She fretted that whatever Rémy had done to save them couldn't be undone.

Oh, get a grip, girl!

She settled deeper into the cushions of Jacob Lawrence's sofa, tugging the tasselled blanket over her head, forcing herself to concentrate on those physical aspects that she could at least control: her thumping headache and her stinging scalp. She closed her eyes and focused on her breathing. She sensed Lawrence's family of figures stealing glances, but in general they ignored her.

Em drifted to sleep. She dreamed again of swimming. This time she dived off the dock at the Abbey into Auchinmurn Bay, where the chill of the sea took her breath away, just the way she liked it when she swam laps round the island and back most summer mornings. The waves buoyed her and her imagination soared, connecting only to the real world in brief glimpses.

Halfway across the bay and there was Zach again. His jeans were rolled up and he was standing in the shallows, waving with the same odd expression on his face that had been there in her previous dream.

56.

NOT ON AN EMPTY STOMACH

'Where's the canvas?' said Caravaggio as he helped Matt to his feet in front of a Monet inside the Orion HQ.

'I left it with Em in a Lawrence painting. It seemed the safest place.'

'Thomas Lawrence?' said Caravaggio. 'The portrait painter?'

'*Jacob* Lawrence. Twentieth century. African-American. You may not have found him yet, but you're going to love him.'

Matt headed into the kitchen. He opened the fridge, grabbed a hunk of cheese and a bottle of orange juice. He gulped the juice and began buttering slices of bread.

'What are you doing?' Caravaggio took a slice of the buttered bread, rolled it, dunked it in the open chutney jar and devoured it. 'We don't have time to cook.'

'I need to eat and so does Em,' said Matt. 'Did you hear anything from your sources while we were gone?'

Caravaggio improvised another sandwich. 'I had other things to do.'

'God, don't tell me,' said Matt. 'Sex?'

Caravaggio smirked. 'Like you, I had needs that had to be met.'

'So you've done nothing since we left?'

'I am well-rested and ready to join the cause.' Caravaggio poured himself a cup of the orange juice and sat at the table. 'And what's happened to our Conjuror? I trust you haven't lost him.'

'Not exactly,' said Matt, layering cheese on to the five slices of untoasted bread and pushing them under the grill. 'He decided to give himself up to the Camarilla.'

Caravaggio sprayed his orange juice across the table. 'He did what?'

'Read the note.'

Matt watched the slices of cheese bubbling under the grill while Caravaggio read Rémy's plan.

'So what do you think?' Caravaggio said, laying Rémy's note on the table. 'Is he strong enough to pull this off?'

For the first time in their brief relationship, Matt sensed concern and compassion from the artist. 'I think so,' he said. 'But it's a big risk and if he fails – if any of us fail – then it's the end of the world as we know it.'

'Such peasant food,' observed Caravaggio, helping himself to one of the toasted cheese sandwiches, as Matt slathered them in chutney and HP Sauce and folded them in half.

Matt wrapped two of the sandwiches for Em in wax paper. 'This is Dunlop Cheddar. It's a delicacy.' He wolfed down his two sandwiches and finished the orange juice. 'Let's go.'

Ella and baby Franklin jumped out of the way just in time as Matt faded in through the purple mirror and collided with the wooden chair. Seconds later, Caravaggio joined him.

Em was on her feet, bouncing anxiously on her heels. Colour had returned to her pale skin and she felt herself break into a broad smile.

'Thank God,' she said, pulling Matt into a fierce hug and grabbing the sandwiches. 'And I'm pleased to see you too, Caravaggio, you bastard.'

'*Cara mia*,' the artist said, 'I am here to help. My quest has always been about redeeming myself and paying for my sins with my own flesh and blood.'

'Up to a point,' said Matt.

Caravaggio pouted. 'It is true that I have kept one or two facts from you all along the way...'

'One or two?'

'... and I am aware that I have not yet proved worthy of your trust, but I will.'

As the artist kissed Em's forehead, she sensed both truths and lies in what he was saying. She wolfed down her toasted cheese sandwiches, deciding to think about that later.

'May I see the canvas?' Caravaggio asked.

Em loosened the tube from her coat sleeve and slid the canvas from the tube. Caravaggio unrolled it carefully. Suddenly Ella was handing baby Franklin to Toby and excitedly taking one side of the canvas, while Jefferson jumped up to hold the other side.

The faceless Reverend Gaines turned towards them, his voice emanating from his chest. 'Ambuya insists that you hang the canvas over the mirror,' he said.

'We have no time for that,' said Caravaggio, keeping a grip on the canvas.

'She insists,' repeated the minister.

Em exchanged glances with her brother. 'Why is the mirror important?'

'It is not,' Caravaggio said. 'Unless you want its extra light to view my masterpiece in more detail.'

Matt and Em spread the canvas on the kitchen table instead, setting aside china plates filled with chocolate cake. Flo pushed her chair out of their way.

'When I became aware of Luca's plans to fulfil the prophecy,' Caravaggio began, 'I took the only measures I could to fight him. I stole this canvas from his bedchamber.'

'Bedchamber?' echoed Matt.

Caravaggio looked sly. 'He is very charming. And stunningly handsome. Difficult for me to resist.'

'I've no words,' said Em.

'That's certainly a change for the better,' said

Caravaggio, rolling the canvas up again. 'Now, there is a little more that I must tell you.'

Em grabbed the canvas. 'Unless it's specific directions to Remy's whereabouts, save it.'

57.

NIGHT SWIMMING

'So now we have the sacred chord, but we've lost our Conjuror.' Em touched her fingers to the scabs that were forming under her hair. She was starting to feel claustrophobic, cooped up in *The Visitors*.

Caravaggio put his hand on Em's shoulder before she left the kitchen. 'This is important.'

'Oh, for f—'

'My dear,' said Flo mildly. 'Language.'

'Luca may actually want me as badly as he wants this canvas.' Caravaggio's voice dropped to a throaty whisper. 'The one person he ever loved, Sebina, was taken from him as punishment for his failure to catch and bring me back to Rome on the day that I was supposed to die.'

Em stared at Caravaggio. 'That would explain why he's so fixated on catching you. It's not just about *what* you stole from him. It's also about *who* you stole from him.'

Did the fact that Luca had loved and lost make him more human? Or had it only served to bury that emotion deeper beneath his demonic nature? Em decided she never wanted to come close enough to the nephilim to find out.

She felt a tug on her jacket.

'Ambuya wants to talk with you,' Flo said, directing Em to the bedroom.

Ambuya patted her quilt. Em sat.

'My child,' said the old lady. 'Don't trust the artist. His secrets are many.'

'We don't,' said Em. 'Believe me.'

She rose from the bed again, but the old lady pulled her back.

'There's more, girl. You've spent the last months resisting the truth that be fermenting in your own mind.'

Em felt the intensity of Ambuya's stare travel beneath her skin and into her mind. The only person who could do that so quickly was her grandfather, Renard.

'I don't know what you mean,' she said uncomfortably, shutting off as much as she could from Ambuya's probing.

The old woman pulled herself up against the white pillow and set her hands on the top of the quilt. 'Lord' sake, girl, I already got most of your secrets when you were asleep. For someone with a mind blessed by the heavens, yo' sure are dumb.'

Em bristled. 'I'm not—'

'Your dreams,' said the old woman. 'You're 'fraid to read them 'cause then you'd have to deal with the guilt that the deaf boy still loves you and you may no longer love him the way you once did. Lust maybe.' She grinned. 'But that ain't love. You may be finding space in your heart for another and it's scarin' you.'

Em leaped up. 'How dare you! How … how do you know about my dreams? About Zach?'

'It don't matter how,' said Ambuya. 'Am right. Ain't I?'

Em exhaled audibly. Ambuya nodded, satisfied.

'You figure out what that boy says to you in them dreams,' she said. 'And then you find our Conjuror.'

'But he's doesn't say anything,' Em protested. 'He just … waves.'

'You sure 'bout that?'

The Reverend Gaines handed Ambuya a cup of water. She sipped, coughed, then looked at Em. 'What you doin' still here, girl?' she said sharply. 'Git!'

Back in the kitchen, Caravaggio and Matt were enjoying huge slices of chocolate cake. Em's head was throbbing as she sat down.

'I need to tell you both something,' she said.

'About time someone else had something to confess,' said Caravaggio, grinning.

The words spilled out of Em in a rush. How Zach had been in her head a lot since they'd returned from Spain, and she'd been dreaming about him off and on ever since.

'But the last two or three times,' said Em softly, 'the dreams have felt more emphatic, more deliberate.'

'And you didn't think that this was important to share?' said Matt.

'Not really. I just figured he'd decided to forgive me and was rebuilding the connection again. Letting me sense his presence like I used to. It's not like we're communicating in any tangible way. It's all vague and kind of ... well, sometimes it's kind of erotic.'

Caravaggio licked icing from his fork. 'I, for one, would like to hear more about those dreams.'

Matt slid his plate away. 'Ignore him. What else do you remember?'

'They always end with Zach waving goodbye,' Em said. 'But Ambuya just forced me to think. What if he's not waving? What if he's signing a message, or a warning?'

'Signing?' said Caravaggio in surprise. 'What is this signing?'

'Zach is deaf,' Em explained. 'He uses sign language. I don't know why I didn't think of it before. I guess ... it's been a long time.'

'Where is this charming Zach now?' asked Caravaggio, tucking his hair behind his ears. 'And why is he sending you messages?'

'He's in New York. He's interning at the Museum of Modern Art, and I don't know why he's sending me messages in my dreams. Maybe he learned something about the Second Kingdom and he's been doing some research on his own to help us?'

'You need to remember what Zach was signing, Em,' said Matt.

Em relaxed, focusing on her breathing, letting her rational mind fade to the background and her imagination take control. She unreeled her last dream like a movie in her head. Back at the Abbey, in the bay, treading water. The sun reflecting off the waves in white light. Zach on the end of the jetty. Signing, not waving. Signing...

She opened her eyes and wrote on a clean page on her sketchpad what Zach had signed.

Hadrian's Tomb.

Caravaggio flinched. 'Rome,' he said uneasily.

Not for the first time since she'd met the artist, Em sensed his fear.

58.

DARKNESS VISIBLE

C rouched over the bedrock of Rome's first citadel, Luca was brooding. The landscape of the Roman Forum, its freestanding Corinthian columns, crumbling walls, broken statues, and triumphal arches sprouting weeds from their foundations, made his mind wander along a dangerous path. What if his destiny was merely an oracle's reckless counsel, not divine prophecy at all?

It had been easy to lure the Conjuror to his lair. His acolyte would be justly rewarded. He knew the Calder twins and the artist – the traitor to his oath and the bane of his existence – would join the Conjuror soon. Yet he was troubled, restless, at odds with himself.

Grabbing a plastic bottle, which rattled in the breeze at his feet, he crushed it in his hand and flung it out over the ancient ruins of the Forum. The bottle's mangled shape whistled across the dirty night sky. In this century, the heavens never truly darkened.

But the skies would darken again when the time came to exact his price for Sebina's pleas as the bronze bull had rolled into the temple, he thought savagely. For every anguished cry when they sealed her inside, when they had wheeled the bull into the temple's fires, they would pay. They would pay, but they would not see it coming.

The spotlights illuminating the Forum flickered as Luca exhaled. The momentary gloom brought out Luca's radiant aura among the ruins, had anyone been looking. Though no one was. The gates had been locked hours ago. And even if the humans saw him, they'd never remember what they'd seen. It was one of the tricks of his kind.

This part of the city had risen from a fiery swamp, an ancient burial ground of the Sabine people. Luca looked across the Forum and saw it as it once had been: triumphant, glorious, proud, packed with the devout and the damned, walking among the divine.

He pushed off the column and walked along what was left of the Via Sacra, which led from the centre of the Forum all the way to the bowl of the Colosseum. He studied the cracked, uneven paving as he walked, shutting out the twenty-first-century traffic to let the voices of his beloved eternal city fill his imagination.

He heard the cries on the night the flame on the citadel was first lit, the army of the Gauls approaching. One after another, Rome's six sister hills ignited their fires, alerting the Republic to the danger. But no one saw

Luca or his kind coming. He recalled legions of Roman soldiers marching in triumph into the citadel, the chants of thousands of spectators celebrating their victory while priests in white robes paraded to the temples of Vesta and Saturn and Jupiter. Still no one was looking at Luca.

Shoving his hands into the pockets of his long coat, he walked past the crumbling grotto where Julius Caesar had fallen. He passed two plebeians pushing carts and picking up the detritus of the day. They weren't looking either.

He stepped off the cracked travertine pavings and on to a grassy knoll, his coat brushing the top of the grass like a breeze. At Vulcan's shrine, two lovers laughed loudly as they scrambled over the closed Forum gate and on to the Via del Corso. Still no one saw him. No one looked at all.

Luca hunkered down to the ground, cracked his knuckles and plunged his hands and arms deep into the earth. The soil sifted through his fingers like water. The blood of martyrs that flowed into the trenches surrounding the Forum consoled him. The voices of the damned sang out to him, lamenting his grief.

Overhead, the spotlights sparked and hissed. Luca fought to keep his humanity buried. He thought of the kind of love he once had. The kind of love that made him impetuous, the kind for which he was willing to sacrifice everything. The kind of love that even after all these centuries he hungered for again. Now his vengeance ran as deep as his love once had, making a dangerous brew. He remained on his knees until the last bulb exploded above his head.

Rising again, he strode down the uneven ground outside the Forum and into the riot of traffic, where multi-coloured scooters swooped round the Circus Maximus like chariots of steel, their riders crowned with helmets instead of laurels. Luca darted among them like Mercury, winged messenger of the gods, sparks flying from the hem of his coat and the heels of his boots, scorching the scooters with the yellow flames and filling their riders with shock and confusion.

In front of Constantine's triumphal arch, he raised his arms, opened his wings and soared to the highest spot on the monument. Perched on the bricks, he pondered the panorama before him. The bones of his city were like the carcass of a beast, its skeleton reaching up through the stones to breathe again. The Forum had once burst with life and teemed with death, its populace taught when to cheer, to praise, to punish. It would be so again. A kingdom of the Eternal. He and the Watchers would make it so.

And then he would exact his revenge.

59.

THE AGONY...

Matt faded into the room seconds after Em and Caravaggio, side-stepping the two of them fast enough to avoid a pile-up, his momentum carrying him across the marble floor on his knees.

When he looked up, his eyes exploded in stinging colours. He tried to grab his shades from his head, but he couldn't make his brain speak to his fingers. Em and Caravaggio were little more than silhouettes across the room.

'Seriously?' he yelled, fumbling for his shades. 'You had to bring us here? The Sistine Chapel? Michelangelo, Raphael, Titian AND Botticelli all in the same room? It's like throwing a vampire on to a sun deck.'

The past unwound like a time-lapse film in front of him. The chapel was in organized chaos. A young boy dressed in a paint-smeared tunic and leggings pushed a wheelbarrow over his toes, the weight of it making Matt howl. Two men in leather aprons ran past carrying buckets of whitewash, sloshing on the wooden platform covering the floor. Matt zoomed helplessly in on a line of apprentices painting the brilliant sky on the curvature of the ceiling directly above him. Four grey-haired elders in fur cloaks and ermine coats stood round a long wooden table spread with cartoons and sketches, passionately debating the blueprints for the chapel's frescoes. A team of young men mixed plaster in wooden vats. Children darted in and out, sloshing buckets of water into a row of troughs where the pews should have been.

The chapel was a cacophony of loud voices, scraping tools and sawing wood, echoing off the covered marble floors. And high above it all, on an ingeniously curved scaffold, stood Michelangelo himself, clad in a loose white shirt and leather trousers under a brown suede tunic. The pockets of his tunic were overflowing with paint rags and scrolls of drawings. He was red-faced and angry, barking orders to boys swarming up and down rows of wooden ladders carrying paint pots, trowels, water buckets and thick brushes to the master. His wavy hair sat high on his forehead and his face was full of sharp edges, cheekbones and a long pointed nose, an effect made even more pronounced by his full sculpted beard.

Matt's eyes were fluttering faster than ever, the images swimming across his vision, but he couldn't stop staring. This was Michelangelo. *The* Michelangelo. The greatest Animare ever known. The Obi Wan of the art world.

Every tableau, every figure, was pulsing, sending streams of colour and light directly to his eyes. It was as if he was absorbing it all. He wiped his hand across his face. Pink tears. Quickly, he pulled off his jacket and held it over his head. The thousands of ribbons of light diffused over him.

I need to get out of here, Em. Em? EM!

60.

...AND THE ECSTASY

Em was faring better than Matt, but only because she was able to perceive the power of the frescoes through the filter of her Guardian abilities. Even so, she found herself sobbing. Matt had dragged himself against the wall, twitching and shaking as if someone was prodding him with a Taser. Em's head hurt from her brother's pain, but the desire to look around overwhelmed her.

She couldn't tear her eyes away from the three hundred *Ignudi* in particular. Michelangelo's nude figures depicted the gods and goddesses whose prophecies and mythologies had shaped Christianity. Painting pagan myths and their heroes in these frescoes was audacious in the extreme, blasphemous, even, to many.

One figure seemed to be whispering to her. A male, muscular and beautiful, his sandy-coloured hair curled at his shoulders, his wings tucked behind his back. His head was bowed, his right hand reaching behind, a garland of laurels linking his space to the figure next to him. Standing beneath the fresco, Em sketched him in a daze, copying him exactly as she saw him.

An icy chill gripped her chest. Slowly, she looked up from her sketch. She felt a combined surge of desire and terror. The figure's eyes were striking and soulful, malevolent and mischievous. His irises swirled with the constellations. As she sketched, he leaned out of the painted space, his hand reaching for her wrist.

I need to get out of here, Em. Em? EM!

The pain in Matt's voice slammed Em back to reality. She ripped her gaze away.

The figure's hand retracted.

61.

STUCK BETWEEN A SATYR
AND A HARD PLACE

Rémy was slowly suffocating. The weight on his limbs and chest was getting heavier and his breathing was shallow and painful. This is what happened when a regular person was bound in a painting. Or maybe not a *regular* person, but someone who wasn't an Animare, anyway.

The soft violin music from the woman in the corner of the canvas was grating on his nerves. Perhaps that was part of the plan. Stuck inside the grotesque painting, Rémy had lost track of time completely and was beginning to lose hope. He was, however, sure of one thing. Whoever had bound him inside this painting hadn't lured him here just to kill him. He could have done that swiftly enough in Chicago. For the first time, Rémy wondered if Luca Ferrante and his sidekick, the dude in the camel coat, might have other plans for him.

'Can you hear me, Conjuror?'

Rémy turned his head with an effort. An old man on a three-legged stool beside the satyr was looking at him.

'I can hear you,' said Rémy, a surge of hope charging through his heavy limbs.

The old man stood. 'I am Tiziano,' he said. 'The artist. Although of course I am merely his image, the representation of his satisfaction with his work.'

'What is this painting?' Rémy gasped.

'*The Flaying of Marsyas*. A foolish satyr who challenged the god Apollo to a contest.'

Rémy guessed the figure gently slicing at the flesh on the chest of the satyr was Apollo. The laurel crown on the young god's head glinted with specs of white paint.

'Guessing he lost,' said Rémy, watching a carving of wet hairy skin fall to the ground from the satyr's hip bone. 'What was the contest?'

'Marsyas found Minerva's musical pipes.' Tiziano gestured to the pipes hanging mysteriously above the gasping satyr. 'And he regrettably challenged Apollo, Minerva's husband, to a contest.' He rubbed his hands together gleefully as more skin dropped from Marsyas. The satyr screamed. Rémy's stomach churned. So did his mind.

'That's a shame,' he managed. 'I believe I could do better.'

Apollo lifted his knife from the satyr's skin and turned his baleful stare towards Rémy.

'You are human,' he said. 'Likely a slave, and certainly

a prisoner in here. Don't be foolish and issue a challenge you cannot possibly fulfil. Your death will come soon enough.'

'If that's the case,' said Rémy with far more confidence than he felt, 'then what do you have to lose?'

The rustling of the fetid wind through the trees and the faint notes of the young woman's violin floated through the barbed seconds. Rémy knew he was in this painting to keep him in a kind of stasis until he was needed. But by then it would be too late for Em and Matt. For Sotto and Two. Maybe for the world. He sucked in more air. It tasted like rotten eggs from the paint. He needed to escape this painting and do what he let himself be captured for in the first place. Destroy Luca and the Camarilla. His choice.

'Don't tell me you're afraid of a black man?' he challenged.

Apollo silenced the woman playing the violin, who let her instrument fall to her side. He reached for the hanging pipes, then walked behind the twitching satyr and faced Rémy where he slumped against the tree.

'I will play,' said the god. 'Then you will play.'

Rémy's pulse raced. He took three quick breaths and tried to calm himself. He squeezed his fingers into a fist. Minerva's pipes had better play just like a harmonica.

'Who will be our judge?' he asked with an effort.

Apollo leaned close to Rémy's ear, his breath cold on

Rémy's cheek. 'I am the son of Zeus, the god of music,' he said. 'I will be the judge.'

'Doesn't seem fair,' mumbled Rémy. 'But hey. One more thing.'

'What?' said Apollo, placing the pipes to his thin pink lips.

'If I win, I keep the pipes.'

62.

WHO'S BURIED
IN HADRIAN'S
TOMB?

'Of all the places to fade to,' said Matt to Caravaggio, his head resting on a tiny round wrought-iron table outside a café across from the Vatican, 'you went for the Sistine fucking Chapel?'

An American family at the next table tutted loudly, scraping their chairs closer together on the narrow strip of pavement and as far away from Matt and Caravaggio as possible.

The artist shrugged, leaning back on his chair-legs, arms crossed. 'Neither of you knew any exit paintings in Rome. I did.'

Em brought out a tray with three lattes and a tomato and basil pizza and plonked them on the table. 'Why not one of your own pieces?' she said. 'Somewhere less obvious?'

'Most of my other works displayed in Rome are much

more visible than you think,' said Caravaggio. 'And the security is often more efficient than in the Vatican.'

'I'm pretty sure the Vatican has state-of-the-art security,' said Matt, diving into the pizza, his shades back on. 'Look at it. The place is a fortress.' In front of them, the Vatican's wall was as high as any castle's.

Caravaggio rolled a slice of pizza and ate it in three bites. 'But the men and women who do the security for the Sistine Chapel have more levels to get through if anything unusual occurs,' he said through a mouthful. 'They would need to go higher up their chain of command before sending in guards to arrest us. I knew that would give us more time to escape. The Vatican is well aware of our kind.'

'I get it,' said Em, mid-slice. 'Because they'd have to find guards aware of what we were.'

'Precisely.'

'Next time, give us a heads up,' said Matt.

Caravaggio bowed his head. 'I'm sorry that I did not consider your unique abilities when we faded, or how they make you both more susceptible to Michelangelo's work.'

Em flipped through her sketchpad to the figure she had copied from the fresco. She slid her pad under the others' noses. 'We need a plan,' she said. 'Look at this.'

Matt reared back from the sketch. 'That's Ferrante!'

'He tried to take me in the Chapel,' said Em, returning her pad to her bag. 'But I think it struck him that he needs your canvas, Caravaggio, before he ... dispenses with us.'

'Either that or he's playing with us,' said Caravaggio. 'Pleasure was always in the forefront of his mind ... and his other parts.'

'How did he track us to Rome so quickly?' Matt asked.

Caravaggio threw some money on to the table. 'Does it matter?' he said. 'Right now we need to save your friend.'

'Fine,' said Em after a moment. 'So where exactly is Hadrian's tomb?'

'The Castel Sant'Angelo. Not far from here.' The artist stood. 'Shall we?'

He strode ahead of Matt and Em, down the hill and into the crowds of tourists milling around the streets.

'You know he's holding back?' said Em, jogging to keep up with Matt's long stride. 'Again.'

'I know,' said Matt.

'And he may be leading us into a trap?'

'I know.'

63.

BE CHILL

Acting lessons had begun when Rémy was a boy. He'd come home from school and his Tía Rosa would be waiting outside the apartment door, ready to pass his mother's care to him so she could go to her evening job at the Chicago Public Library.

'She had a rough day,' she'd say, kissing the top of his head and slipping him his mother's bedroom key in case he needed it.

Annie's daily struggle with reality meant Rémy and his Tía Rosa had worked hard to keep the household on a balanced emotional keel. No drama. No conflict. No friends. Rémy would stand with his back to the door and watch his aunt disappear down the stairs. Without fail, she'd stop and turn and say, 'Be chill,' then blow him a kiss. And no matter how awful his day had been, he'd plaster a smile on his face and go inside.

When Apollo began to play the pipes, Rémy realized he was in even deeper trouble than he'd thought.

He needed to call on all those lessons he'd learned as a boy, pretend he wasn't scared. He had to imagine what the music sounded like and respond accordingly. But inside the painting, it was becoming more and more difficult for him to hear anything except his own raspy breathing. Apollo's music was a faint trickle of sound, washing over him. He forced himself to smile. He nodded. He rapped his fingers on his knees as the god of music played. He needed to appear alert and engaged. He could not let Apollo know that his senses were muted.

64.

THE CASTLE OF
THE HOLY ANGEL

'If these walls could talk,' murmured Caravaggio, glancing round the courtyard inside the high walls of the Castel Sant'Angelo on the right bank of the Tiber. The castle looked like a medieval prison with a cylindrical tower. Its dark, impenetrable walls stood in stark contrast to the white stone of St Peter's Basilica behind them on the Via della Conciliazione.

'They'd say "run for your life",' said Em. 'This courtyard used to flow with the blood of martyrs and fill up with the heads of princes.' She shivered. 'It reeks of death. Let's find the tomb, see what Zach was trying to tell us and why, then get the hell out of here.'

Em was reading the brochure they'd bought at the entrance kiosk. It was still early and the castle, now a museum of ancient artefacts, was not at the top of Rome's list of must-see spots. There was no queue and inside the walls there was only a smattering of tourists.

'The castle is not that old, at least by Roman standards,' she said. 'Emperor Hadrian built it on the foundation of a pagan temple as a mausoleum for his family.' She peered at the map. 'The burial chamber was built underground, directly beneath a hearth flame that burned in a garden at the top of the tower.'

Matt gazed up at the statue that topped the tower. 'A strange place for a garden,' he said. 'Who's the statue?'

'The Archangel Michael,' said Caravaggio. 'There is a story about him and this castle. During an attack on Pope Nicholas's life, witnesses saw the angel draw his sword, swoop into the courtyard and slaughter every member of a cabal about to assassinate the Holy Father, thus saving the Pope's life. The Pope interpreted this as a sign that his reign was blessed, and he renamed the castle for the Holy Angel Michael and reclaimed it as a fortress.'

'It was a sign all right,' said Matt. 'A sign that the Pope had an Animare on his side.'

A tour guide holding a flag on a stick high above her head positioned herself in the queue behind them. Caravaggio smiled at her. She eyed his unusual dress, unkempt hair and mischievous eyes with interest. Caravaggio was about to take her hand and kiss it when Matt cut between them.

'He's busy,' Matt said, and yanked the artist towards the shade of the far wall.

'You can't help yourself, can you—' Em began in exasperation.

The wall behind them exploded, a ball of light flying through the brick. Caravaggio and Matt were tossed into the air, landing on a patch of shrubbery bordering the courtyard. Em screamed. The small cluster of tourists gathering near the gates fled for the street, the last one barely making it through before the fireball tore across the courtyard. The gates slammed shut behind them, throbbing red hot, hissing and sending smoke billowing upwards.

'Are you both OK?' gasped Em, running to where Matt was helping Caravaggio to his feet.

'Scratches only,' panted the artist. 'But we need to get inside.'

65.

MUSSOLINI'S
SAFE ROOM

The massive fireball struck what had once been the Castel Sant'Angelo's portcullis gate, now sealed off within a casing of Plexiglass. The fireball pressed up against the plastic, shifting and stretching itself like a flaming transformer that couldn't decide what shape to become.

The security guards were rushing the tour guide and her party down the emergency-exit stairs. A second wooden door to a downward stairway was barricaded and roped off: *Privato*. No Way Out.

'Please,' a guard shouted at Em, Matt and Caravaggio, gesturing at the exit. 'You must come.'

The flames morphed from a manticore to a centaur in seconds, the human part of the beast naked and covered in scales made of fire. As Matt moved closer, the fireball became a Cerberus: a snarling flaming three-headed dog, a hound of hell. It slammed into the Plexiglass.

Now the guard was yelling in Italian, gesturing at them to move.

'He says a person named Mussolini built a bomb shelter in the lower level,' Caravaggio relayed to Em and Matt. 'This soldier would like us to go there immediately.'

'The tomb is in the lower level too,' said Em.

Matt took his sketchpad from his pocket. 'I'll provide a distraction,' he said, before darting across the stone floor and sprinting up a set of stairs towards the castle battlements.

The guard reached out and grabbed Em, dragging her in the direction of the exit. Caravaggio wound back his arm and punched the guard in the jaw. More shocked than injured, the man let go and pulled his gun.

'Stop!' Em screamed. She took a deep breath and focused on the guard. 'You do not want to shoot anyone.'

The guard wavered. His hand trembled.

'You want to get inside the bomb shelter as soon as possible,' Em told him soothingly. 'Don't worry about us.'

This time, when the amorphous fire slammed against the Plexiglass, hundreds of harpies were forming inside the flames. The surface was melting under the extreme heat. Whatever shape the fireball took, it would be inside soon.

'Get to the bomb shelter and lock the doors,' Em said in a soft voice to the guard. 'And forget what you've seen up here.'

The guard holstered his gun and fled.

'This is Luca's dark magic,' said Caravaggio. 'I may not have mentioned this, but nephilim can control and manipulate fire.'

'Might have been good to know that sooner,' Em hissed.

The Plexiglass imploded. The wooden remains of the portcullis cracked and groaned and a hole opened above the lock. Three fiery harpies with snarling human faces, crow's feet and bat-like wings whizzed through the opening, shooting up to the wooden beams on the ceiling and setting them on fire. Burning wood rained down on Em and Caravaggio before the harpies swooped towards them. One whistled past Em's leg, its wing singeing her jeans. The other two hit Caravaggio straight on, their flaming claws gripping his shirt. He shrieked, clawing at his searing flesh. Em grabbed a chair and smacked the harpies, sending them screaming across the floor.

'To the tomb!' she yelled.

They ran to the wooden door marked *Privato*. Caravaggio kicked hard on the old lock and the door flew open. The harpies screamed louder and charged the door, crashing into it the moment Caravaggio slammed it shut.

'How did you inspirit the guard in English?' Caravaggio panted as they sprinted down the first flight of stairs. The farther down they went, the narrower and more treacherous the stone staircase became. The harpies weren't going to let a wooden door stop them for long.

'It's the message not the medium,' Em replied breathlessly. 'Keep moving!'

66.

GOING UP

On his race to the battlements, Matt stopped at a landing and stared out through an arrow-loop. Police vehicles and two army units were already flanking the front of the castle. Across the Tiber, he could see a string of fire engines speeding their way here. Tourists were keeping their distance. After the initial explosion, most had fled across the pedestrian-only Pons Aelius and were watching from the safety of the left bank. The bridge was empty. The grassy knolls and the cobbled spaces surrounding the castle were cordoned off too.

He gazed down at the courtyard. It looked like a flame-thrower had strafed it. The kiosks were smouldering shells and the burning flotsam of the tourists – backpacks, brochures, camera cases, maps and picnic coolers – lay strewn across the stones like small bonfires. There were no bodies. Yet.

Matt bounded on up the stairs. The fires in the court-yard were distracting witnesses from the fact that although parts of the castle were burning, the fire was consuming nothing. If this was Luca, he was protecting this place for reasons of his own. Not for the first time since leaving Scotland, Matt wondered if they were being tricked, if a plan other than the one they were following to stop the rise of the Watchers and their Second Kingdom was in play.

He sprinted out on to the castle's ramparts, staying low to the ground until he reached the parapets. When he looked over the wall, he realized it didn't matter if he was upright or not. He couldn't see more than a hand in front of his face, thanks to the strange, billowing smoke. He stuck his hand curiously over the wall and into the cloudy mass. It felt hot and sticky, like spun sugar on his skin, and as he yanked his hand back, he saw a burn already blistering on his palm.

The smoke cloud was getting darker by the second. Matt stared up at the great bronze statue of the Archangel Michael, who stood gallantly with his sword on the pinnacle of the tower. Tucking up his hair, Matt started sketching Michael's majestically outstretched wings.

The cloud rumbled angrily and the daylight diminished. Matt gave Michael's chest and arms definition, his legs weight and volume. He captured the gladiator belt and skirt in thick rough lines and, seconds before the sun was blotted out completely, drew the archangel's smooth boyish face.

He scrambled to his feet and looked up at the statue.

Nothing was happening.

67.

GO LOW

The turns were tight and the stairway narrow, making it a challenge for Em and Caravaggio to descend any faster than an awkward jog. The flames raced behind them, but they weren't as nimble as Em. She slowed a little to catch her breath. Caravaggio almost crashed into her.

'If you were any closer, this would be a second date,' she said, pushing him away.

The flames put on a fresh spurt, swooping after them like red crows.

'I hope you know where you're going,' Caravaggio said grimly.

'I think so. Hadrian's tomb is in a vault directly under the pinnacle of the tower.'

A first wave of arrows whizzed round the curve above them. They flattened themselves against the walls as they whipped past. They waited, breathing hard, but no more arrows followed.

'Your brother's distraction must be working,' Caravaggio said.

They sprinted down the last three flights of stairs. At the bottom few steps, they slowed. The ceiling had dropped considerably and even Em, who was shorter, could no longer stand straight. With Em shuffling in the lead, they headed along a tunnel which opened up into a vaulted chamber. The ceiling here was high enough for Caravaggio to stand, but the top of his head was touching the barrels of the vault.

Everything in Hadrian's tomb was covered in concrete dust and screamed of desecration. Frowning, Em lifted the marble head of a gladiator at her feet and set it against the wall. Caravaggio ran his hands over walls that once had been covered in white brick. Only one section hadn't been stripped back to the clay, its gleaming bricks intact.

The chamber was square, and its dirt floor was littered with broken travertine tile and the dismembered bodies of stone and marble statues. Em recognized a head of Zeus, his mid-section sitting in pieces nearby, half a goddess holding a water jug on her shoulders, and against the far wall, a centaur as big as a horse. A rat scampered out of a hole in the centaur's haunches, across the floor and into a pool of water seeping into the ground.

'How is Matt faring, do you think?' asked Caravaggio anxiously.

Em concentrated for a moment. 'He's got things under control,' she said. 'For now.'

They moved reverently around the space, aware of its provenance and worried about what traps they might be walking into.

'This tomb was constructed under the river,' said Caravaggio. He pointed to the coffin in the centre of the chamber, in the middle of four broken columns. 'And that was built directly beneath the vault's keystone. The centre of the Pons Aelius is directly above us. The Romans liked order and symmetry and symbolism in every aspect of their lives.'

The bottom half of the tomb had crumbled to the ground. It looked as if someone had tipped it over. Hadrian's effigy had long since eroded, nose and mouth gone, the only recognizable part being the head wearing a crown of laurels. Caged off from the rest of the room by a rusting iron fence, Em decided the tomb was hardly befitting a Roman emperor whose imperial legions had marched all the way to Scotland.

Her frustration spiked. Why had Zach wanted her to come here?

68.

WALK TO THE LIGHT

Forks of lightning ricocheted from one side of the ramparts to the other. They became one long stream of light, spiralling round and round, rising from the ground at a dizzying speed, until they reached the pinnacle directly above Matt. A radiant mass lit up the heavens with such force it blinded Matt, throwing him backwards into the wall, sending his sketchpad and his shades flying.

The nephilim's wings were folded against his nakedness and his hair was loose around his face. He looked of the light, and yet he had a presence outside of it. He was malevolence personified, and yet fully human in his design. Matt struggled to stand, reaching for his sunglasses.

'Gaze on me,' said Luca evenly.

Matt knew if he obeyed, he would never see again. He squeezed his eyes closed and pressed his back to the wall. The air around him sparked with electricity, his mind an explosion of light and colours.

'Mattie, look at me.'

Matt dropped to his knees and covered his head. It was his dad's voice.

'We will be great together, Mattie. Open your eyes.'

The dad he'd known and loved as a young boy. Not the monster he'd killed among the beasts in Hollow Earth.

'Look at me!'

Matt was seven instead of seventeen. He lifted his head, tears streaming down his cheeks. He opened his eyes.

69.

BATTLE ROYALE

As Matt's eyes fluttered open, the archangel swooped down from the tower with his wings outstretched, blocking the nephilim's light. It was all the time Matt needed. Quickly, he reached for his shades and slammed them on his face.

The archangel raised his sword and charged at Luca. The nephilim laughed. Matt felt the whistling of a fiery spear hit the wall just centimetres from his shoulder. Luca reached for Michael's ankle and whipped the archangel out over the battlements and into the swirling, smoky cloud. Michael darted briefly from the haze, and then he was gone. There was a crash of swords and a spray of dark blue blood. Briefly Matt glimpsed the two creatures – one angel, one half-angel – as they wrestled, Michael hovering above Luca, pushing his blade closer and closer.

With his shaking palms pressed against the walls, Matt sidled round the perimeter of the battlements until his left hand found the automatic plate to open the double doors back to the stairwell. Inside, he pressed the button for the lift, pulled his sleeve over his fist and smashed out the light. The darkness was enough for his eyes to recover their equilibrium. He took out his pad and drew a pair of yellow and black Cyclops goggles right out of *X-Men*.

On the ramparts, the nephilim howled. Hoping the fight was over, Matt crept back to the entrance to the battlements with his goggles firmly in place.

Michael's sword was sliding slowly through Luca's clenched fist, only a touch away from the nephilim's abdomen. The archangel's wings were shimmering, drops of water pooling like shards of glass under his hovering, sandalled feet.

Luca opened his fist. Michael's sword powered into the muscle above the nephilim's hip, but the momentum of the thrust carried the archangel into the nephilim's arms. Luca began to squeeze, enclosing them both in a shell of black, silver-flecked feathers.

Matt fled, taking the stairs three at a time, the archangel's anguished screams tormenting him all the way. He could still hear Michael's tortured cries long after he had destroyed the drawing.

70.

WHY ARE
WE HERE?

Em used a loose railing to dislodge the chunks of marble covering Hadrian's coffin. Another rat scrambled out of the debris, tearing across the room and disappearing into the same pool of water as before.

The tomb was empty.

Em sat on the edge of the marble, her exhaustion taking its toll.

'This can't be right,' she groaned. 'Why would Zach send me a message to come here?'

Caravaggio put his hand on her arm. His sincerity surprised her.

'I have been thinking about the history of this place,' he said, 'and Luca's possible connection to it. What if this is his lair?'

'He's a powerful supernatural being,' said Em, frustrated. 'He's not going to pick this place to hang around waiting for the Second Kingdom.'

A roll of thunder shook the foundations, dropping a chunk of plaster from the ceiling. Caravaggio shoved Em clear just in time. The plaster shattered on the spot where she'd been sitting, as she fell against the part of the wall still lined with the original Roman bricks.

Em caught her breath. She ran her hand over the bricks distractedly.

'Are you hurt?' said Caravaggio, crouching next to her. 'I did not mean to push you quite so hard.'

She waved away his concern. 'Do you know what the mark is on this brick?'

Caravaggio traced his fingers over a worn etching in the ancient brick. 'It looks like a laurel wreath, except it's tiny thistles,' he said intently. 'Masons often signed their work, especially in ancient times. This ring is the symbol of the person who built this vault. Why do you ask?'

'Because I've seen it before.' Em combed her hair from her face, forgetting about the burns on her scalp. 'Rémy found a set of bagpipes back in Scotland. A similar wreath of thistles was etched into the chanter: the part of the bagpipes that looks like a flute.'

She wrapped her arms around her legs, trying to think. What the hell did this mean? She didn't get it. And how would Zach, of all people, know about this place anyway?

Em took out her sketchpad, pressed a blank page over the etching and rubbed her charcoal crayon over the page. 'Do you think it's possible that there's a connection between one of the early Dukes of Albion and the Emperor Hadrian?' she asked.

Caravaggio lifted his head. 'The Duke of Albion?'

Em took out her sketchpad. She pressed a blank page over the thistle etching and rubbed her charcoal crayon over the page. She looked at the transfer.

'The Dukes of Albion were all powerful Guardians. The seventeeth-century one founded Orion,' she said, taking another rubbing, pressing harder to be sure to capture the details on the etching. 'The family has ancient roots in Scotland.'

Caravaggio jumped to his feet. 'What did your seventeenth-century Duke of Albion look like?'

'I'm not sure. Good-looking. Rugged. A lot of hair. They all looked kind of the same.' She shrugged. 'We have a portrait of him at the church, but it's a bit romanticized.' Em looked at Caravaggio curiously. 'Why? What do you know?'

'Please,' said the artist. 'Try to remember the details.'

Em sensed Caravaggio's mind was racing. It felt like she'd just drunk two Red Bulls and a pot of coffee. 'In the portrait, he's wearing a brooch shaped like a peryton at his collar.' Em paused, then added, 'A peryton is—'

'I know what it is,' he said, brushing plaster dust from his trousers. 'And I think I knew your seventeenth-century duke.'

Caravaggio offered Em his hand. She let him help her to her feet. 'I think that duke was my Highlander, the Guardian who saved me from Luca the day I was meant to have died.'

Em's face lit up. 'That means there *is* a connection between this place and Scotland.'

'And,' added Caravaggio, 'I think, perhaps, a connection between your boyfriend—'

'Ex-boyfriend.'

'—and this vault.'

71.

CROSSING
THE TIBER

Another explosive thunder crack shook the foundations of the castle. Matt burst through the narrow tunnel from the stairs.

'We need to get out of here,' he gasped. 'Luca manifested on the roof and almost got me. This entire fortress is stuck in a cloud of his making, like a force field. No one can get in.' He looked at both of them. 'Or out.'

'The rats,' said Caravaggio.

'What about them?' Matt's anxiety was as palpable to Em as if she was wearing a wet wool sweater.

'During my century,' said Caravaggio, 'there was a tunnel running beneath the Tiber that connected this fortress to St Peter's Basilica. For a pope's ... private use.'

The castle shook again. This time the thunderous roar lingered, gradually becoming the warning cry of a raptor to its prey.

'We really are trapped,' Em said, pointing to the passageway. It was completely blocked where a section of the ceiling had collapsed. Plumes of tile dust billowed into the vault. 'It may slow Luca down.'

Matt took out his pad. 'That tunnel better be there, Caravaggio,' he warned, 'because I don't think a pile of rubble is going to stop him.'

Matt drew a big hole in the wall. They all sagged with relief. The hole revealed a long straight vaulted-arch tunnel that looked like the aisle of a church, ankle-deep in standing water, with a lot of wet rats crawling in and out of crevices in the foundations.

The screeching reverberated off the walls as the three of them climbed through into the murky water.

'We have a lot to tell you, Matt,' said Em. 'But first you'd better close up the wall. For old times' sake.'

They smiled at each other. The last time Matt had filled in a wall, the head of the European Council of Guardians' arm had been caught inside it.

In a sizzle of light the wall returned to its original state, with only a faint circle of bluish green remaining where the hole had been. Matt shoved his shredded drawing into his pocket.

Em drew the next animation, creating torches as they jogged through the water. Each step sent dozens of fat rats scattering against the curved walls.

'I hate rats,' muttered Matt, keeping his stride in the middle of the tunnel as much as possible.

They moved as quietly as they could, keen not to broadcast their arrival. The nephilim's screeching grew more muted, but the passageway still shook with each cry.

The water underfoot was turning pink. It was also getting shallower, no longer slopping over their boots.

'Nasty,' said Matt, stopping abruptly.

A mound of half-chewed, dead rats was damming the water. They looked like a recent kill.

'Keep moving,' advised Caravaggio. 'We're getting close to St Peter's.'

They heard music. Rich, round sounds of a violin and a high-pitched reedy instrument in a haze of silver light swirled towards them from a curtain of blackness beneath a carved and vaulted arch up ahead.

'That's Rémy,' said Matt suddenly. 'Conjuring.'

The music was getting faster, more frenetic, full of discord. The haze was hitting the walls around them and breaking the masonry into pieces. The music carried so much pain and anguish and cruelty, it was hard to keep moving.

Em turned to the others, tears filling her eyes.

'Rémy's dying,' she choked.

72.

THE GODS
ARE CRAZY

Apollo set Minerva's pipes down, just out of Rémy's reach. The trees rustled with applause. Shouts of acclaim rose up from everyone in the tableau, except the young woman in pink, who looked grief-stricken. Rémy hoped it wasn't because she had any genuine insight into the outcome. He knew full well that in the myths, the gods always won.

'Are you ready to perform?' asked Apollo.

Rémy accepted the pipes. With a great deal of pain and difficulty, he lifted the instrument to his mouth. He wasn't sure he had enough breath to make any noise, never mind play any notes. He thought he knew what he needed to play, but when he felt the cold bone of the pipes against his chapped lips he changed his mind.

The first notes were weak and dissonant, scratchy and raw. Rémy dropped the pipes. Apollo went to grab them, but Rémy managed to get his foot on them and snatch them up again. The crushing pain in his chest was making it even more difficult to breathe.

He would not be lost to the world this way. With every muscle screaming at him and every breath precious, he put his lips to the pipes again and played a series of chords.

Nothing happened.

Everyone stilled. Apollo leaned forward, the gleam of triumph in his eyes. Then, miraculously, Rémy heard a violin. He turned his head enough to see the young woman in pink had returned her instrument to her chin, and was accompanying him. He followed her lead, catching her melody and mimicking it.

The more he played, the stronger he felt, the more solid his sound, the easier his breathing. The blood dripping to the bucket from Marsyas' body overflowed on to the ground, rushing in rivulets to a river beyond the canvas.

Suddenly he could see outside the painting. Rémy quickened the tempo until he was soaring above the tableau and its terrible cruelty, the thick brushstrokes of the forest and the figures blending together in time with the music. The violin was no longer leading; he was. His tempo grew faster and faster, his pitch rising higher and higher, the painting breaking into fragments of light.

Rémy smelled ammonia and turpentine and blood. Smoke drifted up his nose, his eyes watered and he coughed. The red-hot pipes dropped from his lips and his world faded to black.

73.

FIRE IN THE HOLE

Matt, Em and Caravaggio quickened their pace, trying to reach the mysterious vaulted arch with its silvery haze of music. But their movements felt impeded. They were moving forward, but they weren't getting closer.

'Do you guys feel like we're running into a wind?' Em gasped.

'Or slogging through mud,' said Matt, struggling to lift his feet.

'The darkness,' said Caravaggio. 'I think it's trying to repel us.'

They pushed on, their muscles screaming in pain. The shimmering haze of music was soaring to the curvature of the ceiling, where it blended with the faint echo of the nephilim's screeching. The final two or three steps took them almost as long as the first hundred.

A Latin inscription was carved into the arch.

Matt turned to Em, who was leaning forward, catching

her breath. 'Please tell me this doesn't read, "Abandon All Hope Ye Who Enter Here",' he said.

'"Behold the Way to the Kingdom",' Em translated. '"Through Darkness to the Light."'

The darkness reached for them as Rémy's music turned to silence. The silver haze reddened and dissipated, dropping like bloody tears into the water. Em shoved past Matt. He grabbed her arm and pulled her back before she disappeared through the darkness beneath the arch.

'Em,' he said. 'The nephilim's screeching has stopped too.'

'Silence is often not a portent of good,' Caravaggio said.

Em looked desperately at the artist. 'Do you think Luca's given up the chase?'

'Luca Ferrante has been tracking me for centuries,' said Caravaggio. He glanced back down the long tunnel. 'He's not given up.'

Em shivered. 'At least when we could hear him, we knew where he was.'

Matt gestured at the arch. 'We've got to go through it,' he said. 'There's no other way.'

The three of them stared hopelessly into the blackness. It had weight and depth, and undulated in the damp air. Milton's 'darkness visible': an absence of light.

'Maybe I can see more if I take off my shades,' said Matt.

A deafening whoosh roared behind them. They turned together. The murky water at the far end of the tunnel was rising up into flames, surging towards them. Waves of charred, blackened, screaming rats spewed to the surface.

Caravaggio shoved Matt and Em hard, through the arch and into the dark.

74.

PAINT IT BLACK

'Em? Where are you?' cried Matt, crashing through the sheer unfathomable darkness.

She touched his arm. 'I'm here.'

'Did that bastard just throw us to the wolves?'

A rush of warm air and a surge of limbs slammed Matt from behind, knocking him into a narrow gutter that bordered the bottom of the space. He didn't have enough room to pull himself upright, his hips stuck in the thin trench.

'No, that bastard did not,' said Caravaggio, sounding put out. 'Sometimes you two need encouragement, and those flames were coming fast at us. No one move until we figure out where we are.'

'I'm stuck anyway,' said Matt, taking off his shades and looking at Caravaggio and Em. Caravaggio was to his left and Em was on his right. They both had a thin line of grey silhouetting them, as if the darkness didn't dare come closer.

'The darkness is lighter around your bodies,' he said. 'It's as if you're repelling it.'

'What if this is a trap?' asked Em.

'It doesn't feel like one,' said Matt. 'It just feels ... old and hollow.' The darkness waved like silk around his skin. 'It's like we're in a painted space, but we're not. It's empty inside.'

Caravaggio lifted his boots one at a time out of the gutter next to Matt's legs. When he did, Matt could see the surface stretch like gum on his boot.

'I've never been in a space like this before,' said Matt. 'I can see some indentations in front of us.'

'How do we get out of here?' Em demanded.

Matt could hear his sister's breath getting shallower. 'Calm down,' he advised, squeezing her ankle. 'Do you still have your torch?'

'I dropped it.'

'I dropped mine too,' said Caravaggio. 'But I think I know what we need to do.'

Matt could see the artist gesturing, stretching the silhouette of grey surrounding them all. Matt observed the darkness shifting, the lighter air replacing it.

'I can't see what you're doing!'

Matt took Em's hands and moved them in the same way as his and Caravaggio's. Their gestures lightened the darkness, allowing them to see more clearly the indentations, the dips and dimples in the surface in front of them. They scanned the space, saying nothing.

'It's narrow,' said Em at last. 'But rounded.'

'Sort of oval in shape,' said Matt. He shifted slightly to see the surface in front of him. 'The indentations look like we're in a jelly mould.'

There was a scratching sound, like nails on a chalkboard. Or a knife on plastic.

Or claws on marble.

Em screamed. Caravaggio grabbed her as a wave of flaming rats dropped into the space behind them. They all flailed madly to get away, but the space was too tight and Matt was stuck at their feet. The raptor screeching they'd heard in the tunnel sounded like laughter. Deep and hollow, but laughter nonetheless.

'I hate rats!' Matt roared as the flames died out, and the rats twitched and scratched and bit at him and each other in the gutter at the bottom of the space. There was little he could do except bat them into the blackness. 'The nephilim is playing with us.'

'I know where we are,' said Caravaggio suddenly. 'Listen to me. We need to fade immediately before worse things come.'

The laughter grew louder.

'How do we fade without any art to fade into?' said Em in desperation.

'I think we're inside a carving,' said Caravaggio. 'A frieze. This is bad. This is—'

A blood-curdling screech pierced the void.

'Fade,' screamed the artist. 'NOW!'

FIFTH MOVEMENT

'Cleave the tree down, and destroy it;
before its roots will strangle the earth.'

Book of Songs

75.

DOUBT AND PAIN

Rémy's consciousness returned in a rush of cold air. He shivered and his ears popped. He tried to stand, but couldn't. His hands and fingers tingled where he clutched the ancient pipes, and pain radiated from his right elbow and shoulder as if he'd banged his funny bone.

The young man in the camel coat was staring down at him.

'I can't feel my legs,' Rémy gasped.

'It's a consequence of binding,' said a woman's voice. 'The feeling will return soon.'

Rémy tried to absorb his new surroundings. A vast tree stump stood rooted in the centre of the chamber. It looked as if the top of the tree had been ripped off in anger, yet its roots were alive. Healthy green vines reached across the space and beneath the foundation walls of the room. Shards of wood like pointed teeth stuck out from all sides of the trunk. The head of a half-man, half-ram, a Faunus, with grotesque, twisted features and huge ram's horns, its fur bloody and matted, sat on the stump. The tree's vines were slithering in and out of the vessels hanging from the creature's head, as if the tree was keeping it alive and it was giving life to the tree. Three bronze cauldrons balanced precariously round it, bubbling with a thick silvery liquid.

Rémy crammed Minnerva's pipes into his pocket and pressed his hands on the cracked mosaic tile floor, pulling himself away from the horror. The frame of *The Flaying Of Marsyas* shifted on the wall behind his head.

'Here,' said the woman, offering him a sip of water from a clay bowl.

Rémy turned away.

'It's only water.' She took a sip to demonstrate.

Rémy cautiously accepted and then gulped the cool liquid. He guessed the woman was in her forties, with Caribbean blood in her veins. Her smile lit up her tawny freckled face, making her look much younger. But Rémy had seen smiles like hers his whole childhood. Something dark and tragic lay beneath, and the grief and longing in her voice filled him with sadness.

He took a series of slow deep breaths and scanned the room. The bottom half of the room was wide white brick, and tapestries with richly embroidered figures covered the top half. A faux covering of oak beams held up a crumbling tiled ceiling.

'What is this place?'

The woman made a dismissive gesture. 'If things go according to plan, you won't be here much longer. You've served your purpose, for now.'

The young man in the camel coat seemed tense and impatient, balling his hands into fists at his sides, staring at a glowing light coming from somewhere behind Rémy. It looked as if someone had turned on a television in the darkness.

'Who the hell are you?' Rémy tried.

'I'm Orianna and that's my son,' said the woman. 'The being you know as Luca Ferrante will be here soon. We must leave before that happens.'

Rémy tried to get to his feet, but his legs remained paralyzed.

'The Calders,' Rémy said. 'They don't need to be involved any more. I don't want anyone else to get hurt because of me ... because of who I am.'

'I'm afraid it's much too late for such selflessness.' Orianna flicked her short dark hair behind her ears, revealing a Camarilla tattoo on the inside of her wrist. 'Do you have the canvas with the Devil's Interval?'

'It's in a safe place,' said Rémy warily.

'Keep it that way.'

Rémy felt confused. What did that mean? Didn't these two want it?

Orianna's son ran back into the main chamber, signalling something. He was rolling an unframed canvas in his hands. Orianna slipped a sketchpad from her black leather trousers.

'Your way out is behind that tapestry,' she said, pointing to the opposite wall.

'But I can't fade!' Rémy protested.

'You just did.'

Orianna's son tossed Rémy's harmonica into his lap. Walking to the tree, Orianna reached beneath the ram's head and lifted out an ancient manuscript tied with a gold band.

The room exploded with light. Rémy was tossed into the air as the wooden beams cracked and splintered. A current of energy roared into the small space, knocking him hard against a tapestried wall, sending the harmonica skittering across the tiles. A vine shot across the floor and wrapped up the harmonica before slithering beneath the foundations.

76.

BEHOLD THE ONE

A large portion of the chamber collapsed with an ear-splitting shriek. Rémy howled at the battering of sound. He heard the lamentations of a million voices, the torture of a thousand troubled souls. He heard terror and cruelty and panic and fear. His eardrums popped. Blood trickled down his neck. He covered his ears with his hands, humming softly as he tried to build a barrier in his mind against the onslaught.

The screeching was getting louder and closer. The light pulsed, flooding the room. Rémy glimpsed fire at its core, a swirling shape shifting from flames to wings, the wings sprouting bird-like claws and tiny grotesque human heads. The mark of the Conjuror at the back of his neck began to throb, sending powerful shocks of adrenaline into every organ and a powerful force of energy into Rémy's legs. He scrambled to his feet and ran to the tapestry, tearing it from its golden hooks, desperate to get away before the nephilim fully manifested.

What was on the wall behind the tapestry stunned his mind and his body. Above an altar, bordered on each side with statues of Roman goddesses wrapped in gowns and holding musical instruments – a set of pipes, a lyre – a vibrant marble frieze of a coronation revealed itself.

Rémy could make no sense of what he was seeing.

At the centre of the two-dimensional relief stood a throne: its back made of flailing limbs and monstrous heads with screaming mouths, its seat depicting a crush of broken wings, its legs bursting with the bodies of terrified men and women. And on the throne … on the throne…

Rémy saw himself.

The nephilim stood behind the throne, his enormous wings open behind him. He was anointing the ruler – Rémy – with a crown of laurels. The resemblance was uncanny, down to the precise mark of the Conjuror on Rémy's neck.

Before Rémy could process what he was seeing, a harpy swooped out of the fiery vortex behind him and attacked, gouging the flesh on his arm. Rémy sang out in pain. The note charged like a silver arrow at the harpy, which dropped dead at his feet.

Rémy stared up at the etching above the frieze, struggling to memorize the faded Latin inscription.

Ecce unus est…

Harpies circled overhead, absorbing power from the unearthly fire, shifting and growing to the size of hawks, their human features even more distorted. As they poured into the chamber, the nephilim on the frieze began to pulse with light.

The tapestry hung slack in Rémy's arms. He swirled it around himself, wrapping it around his body, figuring the heavy embroidered fabric would offer him some protection.

The swarm engulfed him. He sang, hitting a series of high notes that pierced the harpies with silver blades, but they kept coming, biting with their razor teeth and stabbing their sharpened claws into his shoulders, tearing all the way to his skin. They were only tearing at his flesh, nothing more. Biting to wound him, to stop him, not to kill him. Rémy punched out more notes. His voice croaked. He dropped a pitch.

There was a whoosh from behind, a sear of heat above his head. A voice, dimmed by his broken eardrums, but familiar. So familiar.

'Rémy!'

He lowered the tapestry. Em was fading into the room from the frieze. He pulled her into his arms before her feet touched the ground.

'Am I glad to see you,' he said hoarsely.

Matt and Caravaggio exploded into the room too, shooting fire extinguishers at the whirling, burning mass behind them. Their efforts weren't destroying the nephilim, but they were at least halting his shape-shifting power. Em stared at the frieze behind her.

JOHN & CAROLE BARROWMAN

'You shouldn't have followed me,' Rémy said.

Em tore her gaze from the frieze. 'That wasn't your choice to make.'

Seeking fresh blood, the harpies fell on Em. Rémy sang out louder and higher than he thought possible, spreading his arms, the tapestry like wings behind him.

Caravaggio's fire extinguisher emptied first. In seconds, the nephilim's maelstrom regained a portion of its lost power. Rémy extended his arms even further, gripping the tapestry and pivoting as he did, protecting himself and Em from the onslaught.

Through the dizzying haze, he saw Luca Ferrante's majestic form rising out of the fiery chaos. The temperature soared, the tiles burned through the soles of Rémy's boots. The harpies combusted. Rémy's voice choked to silence. From the tree stump, the ram's head opened its yellow eyes and uncurled its ivory horns.

Rémy glimpsed Matt and Caravaggio sketching furiously on their open palms. Watched as they lunged across the floor and skidded beneath the cover of his outstretched, embroidered wings. Felt them all turn, and spin, and sink into nothing.

The cold stones of Orion HQ slammed against him, extinguishing the smoke issuing from the heels of his boots.

77.

NOT THE ONE

Three hours later Matt and Caravaggio rocketed out of a painting in the church, landing at Em's feet. A familiar aluminium tube clattered from Caravaggio's hands, rolled to the wall and fell open. *Rest on the Flight into Egypt* unravelled clumsily on the flagstone floor beneath the tapestry, whose embroidered figures were still glowing from the fight earlier.

'Jesus,' said Em, leaping for the painting and cradling it in her arms. 'That's a priceless masterwork, not a boy-band poster.'

'Hmm,' said Caravaggio as he dusted himself off. 'Now. About that.'

Em and Matt exchanged looks. They'd heard that tone of voice before.

'I didn't want to mention this earlier,' said Caravaggio, 'but I'm afraid that I have bad news.'

'What are you going to tell us now?' said Rémy, limping through the door of the kitchen with a plate of toasted cheese sandwiches. Em had fixed the wound on his head with a line of superglue, and so far it was holding well. 'Whatever it is, tell it slow. I can't hear a thing.'

'It's not a masterpiece at all,' said Caravaggio loudly and clearly. 'It's not even my work.'

There was a long silence.

'You mean it's a fake?' said Matt.

'A skilled copy by an Animare,' Caravaggio corrected. 'It fooled me for a long time, but I only fully assessed it while we were inside Signor Lawrence's painting, and I'm sorry, as sorry as you are, especially after all we've been through, that it is not my work.' He accepted the toasted cheese from Rémy. 'Dear God, is this all you people cook?'

Matt rubbed his eyes. 'If I wasn't so exhausted I'd punch you.'

'And if I wasn't so exhausted I'd let you,' Caravaggio agreed.

Rémy sank into a chair with two sandwiches and a can of lager, one of six that Caravaggio had animated.

'So we *don't* have the Devil's Interval?' Em checked. Her whole body felt numb. Was this what Ambuya had tried to warn them about in *The Visitors*? Would the mirror have somehow proved the painting was a fake? 'This means the original painting with the Devil's Interval is still out there?'

Caravaggio nodded.

'Jesus,' said Matt.

'I can't think about that particular problem right now,' said Rémy, rubbing his face. 'It's bad enough knowing a vengeful nephilim and the entire Camarilla are still after us.' He bit into his sandwich. 'Talk me through how you found me in the first place.'

Em opened her mouth, but Rémy held up his hand.

'And when I say talk,' he said, 'I mean use sign language or something. Like the dude in the camel coat. My ears are shot.'

Em felt her skin drain of colour as she dropped her can of lager. It bounced on the table, spilling foam across their research. Matt lunged at the piles of papers and drawings and snatched them up for safety.

'Say that again, Rémy,' said Matt uneasily.

Rémy looked from one sibling to the other. Em looked worse than when the harpy was tearing at her skin.

'The dude in the camel coat?' he said. 'The one in Chicago, at the flat? Good guy, bad guy – I can't work him out. Anyway, he signs. He's deaf.'

Em slumped on to the couch. 'It's Zach,' she croaked.

'Zach?' said Rémy. 'As in, your ex?'

Caravaggio reached across the table and helped himself to the rest of Matt's sandwich.

'Zach can't be with the Camarilla!' Em burst out. 'He wouldn't betray us that way.'

'Of course he wouldn't,' said Matt.

His lie slapped Em like a cold washcloth across her

face. 'If Zach's with the Camarilla,' she said, using her cardigan sleeve to dry her eyes, 'why would he give me a clue where to find Rémy?'

'Maybe because I forced him to take me with him to Rome,' said Rémy. 'I worked out that he wanted to use me, so I offered to go for free if he left you alone. When I left you in the roof in Chicago, I knew I had to get to the source of whatever was causing your pain. I didn't know how else to help you. He had a drawing of you as Medusa. I told him to stop hurting you and I'd go with him. And then, in Rome, I was bound in a painting. Something I never want to go through again.'

'You idiot,' said Em, hiccupping through her tears. 'I would've been fine. I was inspiriting myself. Eventually the snakes would have gone.'

'Good to know that now,' said Rémy, a little irritably.

'When I surrendered, this guy – Zach – kept shaking his head like this wasn't his fault.' Rémy paused and sipped his lager. 'Now that I think about it, maybe he was trying to get me out of there before his mom came back from investigating the safe room.'

Em's confusion was scrambling her senses. She didn't know whether to laugh or cry. She looked at Matt. 'His mom? That can't be true. Can it?'

Matt ran his fingers through his snarly hair. Coloured threads and flakes of paint fell from it. 'We were always told Zach's mom died in childbirth,' he said.

'Clearly not,' said Caravaggio. 'Unless in this twenty-first century you can do what we never could. Raise the dead.'

'He can,' said Matt, pointing to Rémy.

'Do you think anyone else knows about Zach?' Em looked at Matt. 'Vaughn? Grandpa? Anyone in Orion?'

'We'll find out soon enough,' said Matt, a bit grimly.

Em looked at Caravaggio. 'Do you think the chamber with the frieze of Rémy—'

'That's not me,' Rémy snapped.

'—is under the Tiber, or did we fade through that black arch to somewhere else?'

Caravaggio was studying his painting. 'I recognized the frieze,' he said. 'It was excavated from a temple in the Roman Forum during my century. It was believed to be an illustration from the *Book of Songs*. But nothing else about the chamber seemed familiar.' He looked at Rémy. 'Am I correct in assuming you read music as well as conjure with it?'

'No,' Rémy replied sarcastically. 'I make all this music stuff up as I go along.'

'Can you play this?' Caravaggio pointed to the sheet music in the fake canvas.

78.

SOUNDS LIKE TEEN SPIRIT

Rémy slowly reached for his guitar. Caravaggio copied the score on to paper so that Rémy could read it more easily.

'Do you guys really think he should play it?' said Em. 'What if you're wrong and this is the Devil's Interval? We're in no shape to fight right now.'

'It's not the sacred chord,' said Caravaggio. 'The notes are different. It's one of the reasons I realized it was a fake. But I am wondering if it might give us a clue, otherwise why go to all the trouble of changing it?'

Rémy transcribed the notes in his head for his guitar. He scribbled a couple of tabs on the paper.

'Can you play it?' said Matt impatiently.

Rémy stared at the measures for a few seconds more before setting aside his guitar. 'I can play it,' he said, 'but it's not really music.'

He picked up a marker and went to the whiteboard. 'It's a code,' he said. 'My friends and I used to use one like it, to write notes about Sarah Baxter to each other in the band room.' He looked at Matt and Caravaggio. 'She played cello. From a certain angle you could see up her skirt.'

Em threw a cushion at Rémy's head.

'Jeez,' said Rémy with a grin. 'Mind my glued-up head.'

He copied out five bars on the whiteboard, each with five lines and four spaces. Then he copied the individual notes. He left off the clef.

'Music is just a series of symbols,' he explained. 'When you know the cipher – or key – you can transcribe the notes as letters.'

'OK,' said Em. 'So what's the cipher?'

'It's the clef and the scale,' said Matt. He took the sheet of paper from Caravaggio and stood next to Rémy at the board. 'I'm guessing the type of clef tells you which letter is an A or whatever, and you take it from there.'

'It's a bass clef,' said Caravaggio.

'And the scale of C,' said Rémy.

He began to write letters under the notes, erasing two, inverting them, adding two more, erasing them. He scribbled for a few minutes until he had deciphered the message in the music.

Trust a Scot with your whisky but never your women.

Caravaggio laughed aloud. He reached for Em's hand. Wordlessly they ran to the doors.

'Where are you two going?' Matt shouted after them in bewilderment.

'When we were digging around in Hadrian's tomb,' Em shouted back as Caravaggio heaved open the doors, 'we found markings on the bricks that matched the markings on the chanter from the Duke of Albion's tomb.'

Matt and Rémy grabbed their jackets and followed Caravaggio and Em outside. Together, they jogged into the woods, climbing in a line towards the cemetery. The sun was rising over the Cairngorms, and a light autumn breeze was moving in the trees.

'Your Duke of Albion was the Highlander in the carriage on the day that I died,' Caravaggio told Rémy and Matt as they climbed. 'He hinted he was more than just a duke, but I was too close to death to pay attention. When he threw me from the carriage, he took my canvases.'

The door to the duke's tomb at the base of the Martyrs' Monument still stood open. Rémy took the lead, retracing the narrow stone steps deep into the hillside. At the crumbled wall outside the crypt, he stopped.

'The canvas is why the duke had an Animare seal him inside his tomb,' he said. 'For extra protection.'

'I'm getting tired of climbing in and out of tombs,' grumbled Em. 'I need a spa day.'

They clambered inside one after the other. Caravaggio went directly to the whisky barrels. With Rémy's help he dragged one away from the wall. It sloshed. With a shrug, he rolled it towards Matt.

'Hey!' said Matt, jumping out of the way.

There were at least six more barrels to go.

'A little help here,' said Caravaggio.

The fifth barrel didn't slosh. Rémy rolled it in front of Caravaggio.

'Em,' he said. 'Do the honours?'

Em shoved the barrel as hard as she could against the wall. The wood splintered on impact, and sawdust spilled on to the ground – along with a battered leather case wrapped in muslin.

Caravaggio gently lifted the case and set it on top of the duke's coffin. He unwrapped the cotton, then carefully untied the strap of the leather case. Slipping his hand inside, he slowly pulled out his canvas.

'It smells of peaches,' said Em.

Caravaggio examined the true Devil's Interval. 'Must we destroy this?' he said wistfully.

'Oh, man, in a heartbeat,' said Rémy. 'It would take a big element out of the prophecy...'

'I can feel a but coming on,' said Em.

Rémy pulled a face. 'Zach's mom, Orianna. She was very clear about keeping the painting safe, not destroying it. There's more to this than we realize, I think. We should wait until we know more.'

'Then that is settled,' said Caravaggio, kissing Tomas, his angel.

★

Outside, they stood on the hillside and watched the church below light up with strobe lights.

'Looks like Vaughn and the others have faded back,' said Matt.

'I suppose I shall have to throw myself on someone's mercy,' Caravaggio said, tucking the canvas away. 'What about yours?'

Matt snorted a laugh.

Rémy started down the hillside first. 'Friends,' he called over his shoulder. 'Time to go face the music.'

Em caught up to him and linked her arm through his. 'How long have you been waiting to use that line?'

He grinned at her. 'My whole life.'

GLOSSARY

Animare: A person who can bring their art to life, and who can move in and out of art.

Binding: Binding is a kind of suspended animation. Animare are bound into a work of art as a last resort when they lose control of their powers or endanger the secret of their existence. There are secure vaults all over the world containing bound paintings.

Conjuror: The descendant of an ancient African bloodline who has power to alter reality with music and song.

Council of Guardians: A body of powerful Guardians (see below) who enforce the Five Rules for Animare:
1. Animare must not animate in public.
2. Animare must always be in control of their imaginations.
3. If an Animare endangers the secret of their existence, they may be 'bound' (see above).

4. Animare are forbidden from having children with Guardians (see below), as this can result in dangerous hybrids with an unpredictable mix of powers.
5. Children cannot be bound.

There are five Councils scattered around the world.

Guardian: A Guardian has supernatural powers of mind control. A Guardian's ability to influence a person's thinking is known as 'inspiriting'. Council members do not always agree about how Animare should be guided. For example, when hybrid children are created, some Guardians believe that their talents should be nurtured, while others believe that binding (see above) is the only safe course of action.

The Order of Era Mina: The monks in medieval Auchinmurn belonged to the Order of Era Mina. This order had one particular mission: to lock away the monsters of the superstitious past by drawing them into a bestiary called *The Book of Beasts*, thereby reinventing the world as a modern place of enlightenment and learning.

ACKNOWLEDGEMENTS

Like Rémy, Matt and Em, we've altered reality a wee bit in this novel. The *Book of Songs* is our invention, but the *Book of Enoch* is not. We conjured up St Mungo's Castle, the village of Kentigern, the Martyrs Monument and altered the layout of Castel Sant'Angelo, but Peppa Pig and toasted cheese are real. Except for the art under the protection of the Camarilla and Luca's coronation frieze, the other paintings in the story are in galleries and museums round the world. If you'd like to learn more about the art and the music in *Nephilim*, please visit www.barrowmanbooks.com.

Caravaggio lived a remarkable life, and although we've taken obvious liberties we've tried to be true to his temperament, his impetuous and passionate nature, and, of course, his art. Caravaggio's death is shrouded in mystery, but we do know this: he died in 1610 and a few of his paintings disappeared around that same time. Our imaginations fleshed out the rest. If you'd like to learn more about Caravaggio, we recommend Andrew

Graham-Dixon's *Caravaggio: A Life Sacred and Profane* and Francine Prose's *Caravaggio: Painter of Miracles*.

Every book takes a 'village' to create and we'd like to publicly sing praises to ours. Thanks to Lucy Courtenay, our amazing editor, everyone at Head of Zeus, particularly Laura Palmer, Madeleine O'Shea and Suzanne Sangster, and our terrific agents, Gavin Barker and Georgina Capel.

Finally hallelujahs and hugs to our husbands, Kevin Casey and Scott Gill.

With love
Carole and John
2017